FALLING FOR A KNIGHT

THE WILD KNIGHTS

TÉ RUSS

Falling for a Knight

Published by Shanté Russ
© 2019, Té Russ

For Nena.

1

I stepped off of the elevator onto the floor of Gray Towers that housed Zenith Magazine and headed for the receptionist's desk.

When the woman behind the desk looked up and saw me, her mouth spread into a flirty grin.

"Good morning, Mr. Knight," she purred. "Mrs. Gray is expecting you and told me to tell you to go right on in."

I nodded, giving the receptionist a polite smile before I continued to Miranda Gray's office. I gently tapped on the door before I opened it and walked into the office.

"Rome!" Miranda said, hopping up from behind her desk.

"Mrs. CEO," I teased, before accepting Miranda's warm embrace, followed by a playful shove.

"Oh, whatever," she said, with a giggle. "How have you been?"

"I've been well," I said. "And obviously so have you."

Miranda blushed as she rubbed her belly.

"I swear it seems like Spencer keeps you knocked up," I chuckled.

"Shut up, Rome," Miranda said as she made her way back to her chair behind her desk.

"Seriously though," I said, as I sat down. "How is everyone?"

"They're good. Spencer's out of town on business, otherwise he would have been here to meet you."

Spencer and I had gone to the same college and we'd both majored in photography with Spencer graduating a couple of years ahead of me. We'd both done well for ourselves in the field, but after Spencer's uncle had passed away several years ago, Spencer had taken over Gray Communications. I'd been doing freelance photography for him for a few years now.

"Yeah, I hate that I missed him. Hopefully he's around next time I'm here. What about John and Liz?" I asked, referring to Miranda's brother and sister-in-law.

"Liz is prepping for another art show and John is actually going to be a judge on some cooking show competition."

"I heard. Ian is a judge too," I said.

"Oh that's right!" Miranda said. She leaned back in her chair and smiled. "I still can't believe Ian Noble is married."

"I know right," I said, as I shook my head. "Of course now my mother has her eyes set on me and my brothers. 'If Ian can find love then so can you boys,' she says."

"She's right, you know," Miranda said, to which I responded with an eye roll.

"Don't start, Randi."

"What?" she laughed, throwing her hands up. "I'm just

sayin'. All the Nobles have found the loves of their lives. Maybe it's the Knight brothers' turns."

"Bite your tongue, woman," I said, with a grin as I reached into my pocket. "How 'bout we get to the real reason I'm here."

I pulled out an SD card and slid it over to Miranda, who took it and put it into her computer.

"Shit, Rome," she gasped. "These pics are...stunning."

"Well...you know," I boasted. "I try."

"I can't thank you enough again for taking on this job for me. And at the last minute. We've got some great photographers here, no doubt. But none of them could have captured this the way you did."

"I appreciate your confidence in me, Randi," I humbly replied.

We chatted for a few more minutes before we both stood and Miranda walked me to the elevators.

"So, where are you off to now?" Miranda asked.

"Vacation," I said as I pressed the button to the elevator.

"Well have a great time. And I know I don't have to tell you to take plenty of pictures," Miranda said with a wink as the elevator doors opened.

I stepped onto the elevator and turned to Miranda with a smile. "You already know."

"*Cynnnnnthiiiiiiaaaa,*"

The whiny drone of Priscilla's voice made me cringe and slam my notebook shut. I looked at the time on my laptop.

*Just a few more hours...*I reminded myself as I stood and ambled to the other side of the apartment.

"Yes," I said when I arrived to where Priscilla was being fawned over by her makeup team.

"Can you be a dear and run over to that quaint little juice bar and get me a smoothie bowl?"

"The one that's damn near an hour from here?" I said, with a raised eyebrow.

"Yes."

"I'll have Lily take care of it," I said, turning to go and find the other personal assistant who helped me keep up with Priscilla's day to day tasks.

"No!" Priscilla cried. "She never gets my order right. It's bad enough you're leaving me alone with her for a week so you can go on your little girl's trip."

"A trip that I have to leave for the airport soon," I reminded her.

"Cyn! Please!" Priscilla begged, sticking her lip out in an annoying pout.

Desperate to avoid having to deal with one of her epic tantrums if I said no, I blew out a sigh, as I said, "Fine."

"Thank yoooou!" she sang.

I rolled my eyes and took off. I ran into Lily as I made my way to the front door.

"Are you headed out for your flight?" she asked, doing a shimmy that made me smile.

"Not yet," I said. "The princess wants a smoothie bowl."

Lily's eyes widened.

"At that place damn near an hour away?!" she balked.

"That's the one," I said, checking my purse to make sure I had everything.

"Cyn," Lily insisted. "I can go get the smoothie bowl."

"It's fine," I said. "You're going to have to deal with her by yourself for the next week. I can handle this one last errand."

"But you've got to get to the airport."

"I'll make it in time," I assured. "There's no way in hell I'm missing my flight."

I damn near missed my flight.

All because of a goddamn smoothie bowl.

That really had me pissed off. Because I was meticulous when it came to my schedules. And because I couldn't say no to 'her majesty' when I had a perfectly good co-executive assistant to help me deal with Priscilla, my schedule had been completely thrown off.

Now here I was in a full sprint through the airport with my rolling carry-on bag, praying to God that I'd make it to the gate before they shut the doors on me, while my two best friends, Jaclyn and Octavia, were frantically texting me.

Jay: Bitch...where the fuck are you? You'd better not miss this flight.

Tay: She's not gonna miss the flight, J. Chill.

Tay: But seriously tho. Where the fuck are you?

I ignored their texts and kept running. When I saw my gate number, a sense of relief flooded my body. I made it!

That relief was quickly doused when I saw the gate attendant reach for the door.

"*Wait!!*" I screamed at the top of my lungs, causing a crowd of people to turn and look my way. Thankfully one of the people was the gate attendant.

When I saw her shaking her head, my heart stopped.

"You barely made it ma'am," she said, opening the door. "Boarding pass."

I quickly lifted my phone, which had my mobile boarding pass on it and waved it on the scanner.

"Enjoy your trip to Trinidad, Miss Tremaine," she said with a sympathetic smile.

I knew I must have looked a mess, but I didn't give a damn.

I'd made my flight.

I was officially on vacation.

I was enthusiastically greeted by Jaclyn and Octavia, who pulled me into a quick group hug after I shoved my carry-on into the overhead bin.

"I knew you were gonna make it," Octavia said, as I squeezed past Jaclyn to my seat in between the two of them.

"What had you so damn late?" Jaclyn asked. "I just *knew* your ass was gonna be here three hours ahead of the boarding time."

When I released a frustrated sigh, I heard a collective groan from Jaclyn and Octavia followed by both of them saying, "Princess Priscilla."

"You seriously need to quit," Octavia said with a shake of her head.

"You know it's not that simple, Tay."

"Sure it is," Jaclyn argued. "You just tell that bitch you're done being her doormat."

"Jay—"

"She's right, Cyn," Octavia interjected.

"Look. The whole point of this trip is to *not* discuss my current employment situation. So can we just...drop it?"

"Yeah," Jaclyn said. "We'll drop it. For now."

"Thank you," I said, as I buckled my seatbelt after the flight attendant politely motioned for me to do so as she walked by.

Soon the plane was taking off and I settled in to enjoy the five hour flight to Trinidad and Tobago.

When the flight attendant came by to take our orders, we all opted for wine. When she came back with our glasses we all held them up and toasted.

"Carnival, here we come!" Jaclyn exclaimed and Octavia and I clinked our glasses with Jaclyn's before downing our wine.

After attending the Labor Day Carnival parade in Brooklyn the year before, Jaclyn, Octavia and I agreed that our next girls' trip had to be Trinidad and Tobago during Carnival.

We'd started these trips in college. Jaclyn and Octavia had whisked me away to Mexico as a way to help me cope with the sudden and tragic loss of my father my junior year in college. Somehow it morphed into a yearly tradition that we'd managed to keep up over the last decade.

I glanced down at the charm bracelet on my wrist – a gift from Dad – with a smile and then reached under the seat in front of me and pulled my notebook out of my bag. I flipped through the pages until I found the sketch I'd been working on earlier in the day before Priscilla had interrupted me to go on that stupid errand for her.

"Cyn," Octavia gushed. "This looks amazing!"

"Thanks, Tay," I said, as I started working on the drawing again. I'd gotten so wrapped up in it that I was shocked when the pilot came on the intercom and announced that we'd soon be making our descent to Piarco International Airport.

After wading our way off the plane, through customs and finally baggage claim, we grabbed a taxi and gave the driver the address to the home we'd rented out for the week.

We ooh'd and ahh'd during the entire drive, taken in by the sight of beaches that went on and on for miles.

But when we arrived at our rental, we were even more amazed.

"Damn Cyn!" Jaclyn said once we were inside and put our bags down. "This place looks even better than the pics you sent us."

"It does," I agreed, as I pulled my phone out and went to my planner app. I had our entire trip planned down to the minute. I didn't want to miss a single–

"Hey!" I shouted as Jaclyn snatched my phone from my hands. My eyes grew wide as I watched her swipe through deleting everything. "Jay! What the hell?"

"You are off the clock, sis. Now is the time to be free of all that scheduling bullshit," Jaclyn told me with a serious face.

Octavia came to stand next to Jaclyn, three shot glasses filled with some brown liquor in them. She nodded her head in agreement with Jaclyn as she handed us each a glass. "That's right. This trip is about living in the moment, not living in that dumb ass planner."

I stared at them for a moment and then let my shoulders fall. Partly in acquiescence and, if I was being completely honest with myself, partly in relief. Spontaneity was such a rarity in my life these days that I'd kind of forgotten what it was like to just let my hair down and have fun.

That's why these trips with my girls was *so* necessary.

I needed to be reminded that there was more to my life than Priscilla Tremaine – the spoiled little stepsister that my father had adopted when we were young girls after our parents got married.

"Okay," I said, as I lifted the shot glass to my mouth. "No schedules. Just...living in the moment."

2

"Cyn...Cyn wake up, it's time to start getting ready."

I groaned and tried to pull the covers over my head, but Jaclyn wasn't having any of that.

"Get. Up," she ordered, as she snatched away my blanket.

We'd gotten up at three a.m. on Monday morning to go and head over to J'Ouvert. We'd partied well past the break of dawn, before coming back to the house, where I'd passed out – my entire body covered in paint – for a couple of hours before I got up showered and we were off again, to party well into the night.

I thought I'd be able to sleep in a little on Tuesday, but obviously I was wrong since Jaclyn was practically dragging me out of the bed.

"I've got to do your makeup," she insisted, while tugging my ankle.

"Fine," I growled as I finally got out of the bed.

Half an hour later, I walked out of my bathroom and stopped in my tracks.

"What the hell is that?" I asked as I stared at the outfit hanging on my bedroom door.

Or lack thereof, really.

The bikini left nothing to the imagination. It was just several pieces of string with just enough fabric and sequin to barely cover up my boobs and pussy.

"It's your costume," Octavia said enthusiastically, as she shoved a drink into my hands. That seemed to be the theme of this vacation: Keep Cyn Drunk.

Never mind the fact that it was nine in the morning.

"You don't honestly expect me to go out in public with my ass and titties just out there for the world to see," I argued.

"Why not?" Jaclyn asked. "*Every*body else is. No one is gonna think anything bad."

"Quite the opposite," Octavia added. "Cyn, your body is bangin'! You better show it off and see if you can find you a Winston Duke out here to blow your M'baku out."

"You did *not* just say that shit to me," I said, falling into a fit of giggles as the liquor began to loosen my reservations about the costume.

I had to admit, it *was* gorgeous.

Live in the moment, Cyn, I reminded myself – had been *constantly* reminding myself over the last few days that we'd been here.

I snatched the outfit off of the door before I could change my mind, and several minutes later stepped out of the bathroom to Jaclyn and Octavia squealing and whistling at me.

"Let us help you get your wings on," Jaclyn said, hopping up from the bed.

Surprisingly, the wings weren't as heavy as I'd assumed they would be and neither was the matching headpiece.

"Yasss bitch!" Octavia said, snapping her fingers at me. I turned and looked at myself in the mirror and *damn...*I did look good.

I'd decided to leave my hair down, the tight ringlets cascading around my face down to my shoulders.

"We'd better get out of here, so we can find our band," Jaclyn said, as she looked in the mirror and adjusted her top.

I slid my feet into my tennis shoes, double-knotted the strings and grabbed the fanny pack off the bed and we left the house.

Things were in full swing by the time we arrived, but we didn't have a hard time finding our group and they gave us a warm welcome. The energy was infectious with the soca music blasting and bodies writhing and wining all around us. Those elements mixed with my lowered inhibitions thanks to what-ever drink Octavia had gotten for us off of one of the trucks had me feeling better than I'd felt in ages.

For most of the parade I stuck with my girls, dancing and laughing in the streets. A flash in the distance caught my atten-tion and when I looked up I noticed a camera pointed directly at me.

Something stirred inside of me at the sight of whoever it was obviously taking my picture. I couldn't see his face but judging from the rest of him...*damn.*

He wasn't dressed in an opulent costume like a lot of people in the parade; instead he opted for a simple white tee and shorts. Even still, he somehow managed to stand out in the crowd. Tall, with warm chestnut skin and locs that were pulled back and stopped right above his shoulders. My eyes drifted to his arms, muscles that flexed every time he moved to take a photo.

He was holding his camera at a vertical angle which gave

me a peek at his full, sexy looking lips. Which had tilted up into a knowing smirk.

He'd caught me checking him out.

Typical Cyn would have been embarrassed and would have quickly found something else to focus on.

But vacation Cyn was a bit bolder.

So instead, I struck a few poses for him, which cause that sexy smirk of his to widen.

I continued posing and dancing as we moved closer and closer to where he was, slightly off to the side of the parade.

When I reached him, he finally brought the camera down from his face and my breath stalled in my lungs.

The man was even more gorgeous than I could have possibly imagined.

We stood there staring at each other for a moment, until a couple dancing behind me, bumped into me, causing me to lurch forward.

Thankfully, Mr. Cameraman was in arm's length and reached out and caught me, making sure I didn't fall.

"You good?" he asked, looking me up and down.

I nodded, not trusting my voice. His hands were around my waist and his touch had my heart pounding in my chest.

I brought my drink up to my lips, sipping out of my straw as I started back dancing, my hips swaying from side to side.

Dancing with complete strangers was nothing out of the ordinary and he obviously was down because he tightened his grip on my waist and began moving with me. I turned in his arms, bent over and wined on him with everything in me.

I could hear Jaclyn and Octavia somewhere cheering me on, so I kept right on dancing with him. I turned to face him again, lifted my leg and hooked it around his waist and rolled my body against his. He grabbed my thigh to keep it in place, his fingers digging into my skin and his other hand was on my bare ass.

I looked up to find him staring down at me, a thin sheet of sweat coating his forehead.

Eventually, I extricated my body from his.

"Thanks for the dance," I shouted as Jaclyn and Octavia dragged me off to continue making our way through the parade.

"The pleasure was *all* mine, gorgeous," he shouted back.

"Damn!" Jaclyn said, once we were further along. "Brotha was super fine."

"Yeah he was," Octavia co-signed. "Y'all damn near made a baby in the middle of the street the way y'all were all over each other."

"Oh shut up," I giggled, but couldn't help but fan myself at the memory of us dancing together.

I'd danced with plenty of people so far, but dancing with him had been...different.

I couldn't explain it, but even though we'd barely spoken to each other, there'd been a spark that was undeniably palpable.

I looked over my shoulder, hoping I could get another glimpse of him. Unfortunately, he'd gotten lost in the crowd. He was probably back to taking pictures or dancing with other women; my dance with him already becoming a distant memory.

For some reason, that disappointed me a lot more than it probably should have.

"Goddamn..." I whispered under my breath. It was the day after Carnival and I'd dipped off into one of the local cafes for lunch. But I could barely focus on my food as I sat and looked at my camera screen, scrolling through picture after picture of the woman who was easily the baddest chick I'd seen in longer than I could remember.

I'd taken photos of more women than I could count during the parade, and all of the other preceding events that had led up to it; but there was something...completely captivating about her.

I'd spotted her long before she'd realized that she'd become the latest subject for my camera.

She looked tantalizing in her costume: a gold bikini covered in rhinestones and sequins that showed off damn near every inch of her body. A body that was simply...

Goddamn...

And the contrast of matching wings and headdress – a vibrant mixture of orange, yellow and red – against her pecan colored skin was absolutely stunning.

But it was her smile...Her smile was enigmatic as she danced her way down the street with her homegirls, stopping occasionally to take a photo or video with her cell phone.

I couldn't take my eyes off of her.

And when she finally noticed me and made her way over to me...and we shared that brief, yet highly electric dance together...

Goddamn...

Just the memory of her supple skin, my hands on her soft ass had my fingers twitching.

I pushed my camera away and grabbed my coffee cup, shaking my head with regret.

"You should have at least gotten her name, you fuckin' idiot," I mumbled under my breath as I took a sip of my drink.

The bell over the door to the cafe rang and out of sheer

reflex, my gaze drifted over to that direction for a brief moment.

But then I did a double take, damn near choking on my coffee, when I saw who'd just walked in.

It was almost as if I'd conjured up the woman in my photos that I'd just been thinking about.

She looked just as good today as she did yesterday in her denim shorts and tank top. Her hair – that I'd admittedly imagined gripping while doing unspeakable things to her body as she'd provocatively wined her ass on my groin – was piled on top of her hair in a messy bun and she was wearing a large pair of sunglasses.

I watched as she slid into a booth on the other side of the cafe and gave the waitress who came to her table her drink order.

Once the waitress left I stood, grabbed my camera and immediately headed over to her table where she was still looking at the menu.

As if sensing my approach she lowered her menu and she let out a little gasp when she recognized me.

"You..." she whispered, her eyes wide.

"Hello again," I said, grinning at her.

"Hey...hi...hello..." she stammered.

"Did you enjoy the rest of Carnival?" I asked.

"Oh...yes, I did."

"Good."

"Did...you um...get a lot more pictures?"

"I did...but I don't think any were as good as the ones I got of my best dance partner of the day," I replied, causing her cheeks to darken.

"'Scuse me, handsome."

I stepped to the side to allow the waitress to set the coffee down on the table and she looked up at me and asked, "Yuh movin' ova here?"

I looked down at the woman and asked, "If the lady isn't expecting anyone else and doesn't mind."

"Yes...I mean no! I mean..." She paused, exhaled and looked up at me again. "No, I don't mind. And I'm not expecting anyone else. Please, sit."

The waitress gave me a knowing grin as I sat down. "Please put her order on my check," I said to the waitress once she'd taken the woman's order.

"Oh, no. That's not necessary..." she tried to argue, but the waitress had already taken off. "You didn't have to do that."

"I know, but I'd like to," I insisted.

"Thank you..." Her mouth hung open for a moment and then she clamped it shut, shaking her head. "I don't even know your name."

"My friends just call me Rome," I supplied.

"Rome," she repeated.

"And what is your name, gorgeous?"

"Cynthia. But you can just call me Cyn."

It was quite appropriate honestly. The way she'd ground her body against mine yesterday was absolutely sinful. But I wasn't about to say that out loud because the play on words was a bit corny.

"It's nice to officially meet you, Cyn," was what I opted with instead.

"Likewise," she said, as the waitress returned with Cyn's order.

"Where are your friends I saw you with in the parade yesterday?" I asked. The three of them seemed to be joined at the hips during the parade; except for those glorious few minutes that Cyn had separated herself from them to dance with me.

"They decided to go on some excursion," Cyn said, as she cut a piece of her food with her fork. "I needed a day to just...chill. But then I got hungry and realized there wasn't really anything to eat at the house we're renting. I found this place and saw it had good reviews so I decided to check it out."

"Cool. How's your food?"

"Amazing," she said. She looked around the restaurant. "It's kind of strange seeing everything so…"

"Normal after partying for days on end?" I finished.

"Yes!" shaking her head, she added. "I swear I don't think I've ever partied or drank so much in my entire life."

I sat back in my seat and chuckled.

"Yeah, that's Carnival for ya."

We sat in silence for a moment and I watched as Cyn's eyes landed on my camera. "Sooo the pics you took of me yesterday are on there?"

"Yup."

"May I see them?"

"Of course," I said, turning my camera back on. "And just so you know, since I didn't get a chance to get your permission yesterday, I wouldn't have posted them."

"Oh. That's um…thank you," she said, before I slid the camera over to her.

Once I showed her how to scroll through the pictures, I sat back and watched her as she looked at picture after picture of herself.

"You took…a lot of pictures of me."

"The camera seemed to be taken by you."

"The camera…or the cameraman?" Cyn asked, looking up at me.

"Maybe a bit of both," I freely admitted.

She gave me a nod of understanding and went back to looking at the pictures of her.

"Wow. I look…so happy."

My brows furrowed at her words.

"Yeah, you do. But why do you seem surprised by that fact?" I asked.

She shook her head. "It's nothing."

"Doesn't sound like nothing."

I watched as she pulled her bottom lip between her teeth and nervously gnawed on it.

"I know we've only known each other for a whole two minutes, but...you can talk to me, Cyn. Sometimes it's easier talking to a stranger."

She looked out of the window and let out a huff.

"Life has just been...rough over the last few years. I can't stand my job. I lost my father eight years ago, and the wound still feels fresh as if it happened days ago. And don't even get me started on my stepmother."

"Cyn, I'm sorry," I said, reaching over to touch her hand.

"No," she said. "I'm sorry. I didn't mean to dump all of that on you all of a sudden."

"Don't trip about it, gorgeous," I said. "And for what it's worth, with all of that going on in your life I'm glad that you seemed to enjoy yourself a lot yesterday."

"Thanks in part to you," she said quietly.

"Is that a fact?"

She had this shy look on her face as she tucked a loose curl behind her ear and said, "I mean...for a brief moment."

"So...what's a brotha got to do to elongate that moment?"

"What did you have in mind?"

"I'd like to take you somewhere. It's one of my favorite places on the island."

"Are you from here?" she asked. "Because you sound–"

"American?" I finished. "Yeah. Born and raised in the states, but my father...He was from here."

"Oh...*Oh!* Rome, I–"

I held up my hand. "It was a long time ago. But yeah that shit about it still feeling like a fresh wound. I get that."

The waitress brought the check and I scooped it up and handed her my debit card to pay for our meals.

"So, what do you say?" I asked. "You up for a lil adventure today?"

"Oh...Rome, I don't know," she hesitantly replied.

"Look, Cyn," I said, pausing because I knew what I was gonna say could come off as cheesy, but fuck it. No risk, no reward, right? "This could totally be one-sided, but something tells me it's not. Yesterday, when we danced...there was *something* there. Some kinda spark, I'm pretty sure you felt it too. I could see it in your eyes. Something drew you to me."

She looked down at the table.

"I fly home tomorrow."

"Then just give me today."

I don't know why I felt so fucking desperate to spend time with this woman; but I wasn't ready for our time together to end.

"Live in the moment with me today, Cyn."

That caused her head to shoot up.

"What did you just say?"

"Live in the moment with me...?"

"Okay."

"O–Okay?" I repeated, slightly shocked.

"I'll go with you," she said, nodding. "But I'm sharing my location with my friends."

It was the responsible thing to do. She was on an island about to go off with a strange man. I stayed on my mother who was constantly traveling with my aunt to foreign places to make sure she shared her location with me and my brothers.

"Sounds good to me," I said, standing and holding my hand out to her. "You ready to go?"

I watched as she hit the button to share her location and then nodded and reached up to place her hand in mine.

"Ready."

3

Jay: Bitch, WHERE TF are you going?!?!

That was the text she'd sent me after I shared my location with Jaclyn and Octavia on the tracking app on my phone. I still had to use *some* common sense.

I peeked over at Rome who was driving and bobbing his head along to the music playing softly on the radio and then turned my attention back to my text messages.

Remember the guy I was dancing with at the parade yesterday?

Tay: That FINE ass with the camera?

Yes.

I went on to tell Jaclyn and Octavia about how I'd ended up in the same cafe as Rome; after those bitches ditched me to do some swimming with sharks shit they *knew* I wasn't gonna be down for. Yeah, I was livin' in the moment, but I had to draw the line *somewhere*.

I'd been hesitant to go with Rome at first, Typical Cyn telling me all the reasons why it was a bad idea. But then he'd said Vacation Cyn's mantra and I knew I couldn't say no.

Rome had been right, something *had* drawn me to him at the parade; and it wasn't the liquor.

Jay: If you don't ride that man's dick until sunup, we're leaving you in Trinidad.

I swallowed a laugh and looked over at Rome again.

It *had* been a while since I'd been with a man. Truth be told, while dancing with him, I'd gotten a bit of a sneak peek at what Rome was working with and...

Goddamn...

Maybe Jaclyn had a point.

Octavia merely backed up Jaclyn's advice with a simple text of **Be safe and shoot us an S.O.S. if shit is foul. We'll come and get you.**

Will do. Love you, I replied back and then tucked my phone away to look out the window as we drove down a winding road that overlooked the ocean.

"Wow," I sighed. "This is beautiful."

"Yeah," Rome agreed.

"Earlier at the cafe, you said your father was from here. Did you get to visit here often?"

"Every summer and occasionally during the holidays," Rome said. "We didn't get out here as much after my father passed. But my brothers and I try to visit at least once a year. Our grandmother still lives here."

"How many brothers do you have?"

"Two. We're triplets actually."

"Really?"

"It kinda runs in the family, multiples. My mother has a twin sister."

"Wow!"

We drove for a little while longer, and eventually Rome turned down a dirt road surrounded by trees. Soon he came to a stop and turned the car off.

"We'll have to walk from here," he said. "But it's not too long of a trek."

"Okay," I replied, before he got out of the car and came around to my side to help me out.

He kept my hand in his as he guided me through the forested area. We'd only been walking for a few minutes when he stopped and turned to face me, a sexy grin spreading across his lips.

"Are you ready?" he asked and I responded with an eager nod.

He led me through a clearing, and my mouth fell open in awe at what was easily one of the most beautiful beaches I'd ever seen.

"Rome...this is..." I couldn't find the words to properly describe my thoughts.

Rome squeezed my hand a little tighter and pulled me further towards the beach.

"Come on," he said.

He toed off his shoes, and I did the same, loving the way the powdery soft sand felt beneath my feet.

I looked one way down the beach and then the other realizing, "There's no one here."

"Yeah," Rome explained. "Since it's not as easily accessible as so many of the other beaches it's stayed fairly secluded."

"I see why this is one of your favorite places," I said, releasing his hand. I kept going until I reached the shoreline. The ocean water splashed against my toes and I leaned my head back and shut my eyes, taking in the feeling of the sun warming my skin.

I stood like that, enjoying the sound of nothing but waves, for several minutes; until I heard a beeping from behind me.

I opened my eyes and looked behind me to find Rome, camera in his hand, taking pictures of me.

"I didn't even realize you'd brought that with you," I said.

"I pretty much always have a camera with me," he said, taking another picture. "You don't mind, do you?"

"I suppose not," I said, scrunching my nose.

The sound of the shutter clicking as he took several more pics filled the air, and he said, "I told you earlier, the camera seems to be taken by you."

"Hmmm." That hadn't been the only thing he'd admitted to being taken by me. Instead of bringing that up again, I said, "It just feels kinda strange, that's all."

"Having your picture taken?" Rome asked, lowering his camera. "Why?"

"In my line of work...hell in my life...I guess I've just gotten used to being invisible. My job is not to be seen."

"That's quite a shame," Rome said quietly. "Because you're definitely worth being seen."

"Not everyone thinks so."

"Fuck everyone who doesn't."

His words made me look up at him and I found him staring at me.

"*I* see you," he said.

His gaze was so intense that I had to look away. Desperate to change to subject before I got all emotional over his words, I turned my gaze back to the water and asked, "How did you find this place?"

When I realized he was no longer taking pictures of me and that he'd taken a long time to answer, I turned to look at him.

He had a sad smile on his face when he finally answered. "My dad used to bring me here as a kid."

"Oh."

"Being a triplet, there was always this...assumption that we always did everything together. And I mean...we kinda did," he chuckled. "But my dad made sure to spend time with us individually too. And this is where he'd bring me. He taught me a lot of shit out here. I make sure to come out here whenever I visit the island."

"And you brought me with you this time?" I asked.

Rome nodded. "You mentioned being unhappy and missing your father. Coming here brings me peace." Shrugging, he added, "I figured it might do the same for you."

I turned my gaze from him back to the ocean.

"It does," I whispered.

We sat down in the sand and talked forever; trading stories of our fathers that brought smiles to both of our faces.

"Thank you for bringing me here," I eventually said. "This...has helped. More than you know."

"You're welcome, gorgeous," he said as he turned towards me and pushed a strand of hair out of my face. When his thumb lightly grazed my cheekbone, my eyes drifted shut. His hand slid to the back of my neck and he gently pulled me closer to him, giving me ample time to stop him or back away, if that had been what I wanted.

It wasn't.

I closed the little bit of distance left between us, and eagerly lifted my head as he slowly pressed his lips against mine. It was a soft kiss, that had me melting against his body. He kissed me again, and again, each time a little deeper, until I opened my mouth and sucked his tongue into my mouth, causing him to let out a moan that had my entire body shivering. He grabbed me by the waist and pulled me so I was straddling his lap and I wrapped my arms around his neck.

Finally, the need to breathe forced us apart, but Rome kept his hands around my hips. He dropped his forehead to mine, his chest rapidly rising and falling.

"Goddamn, woman," he said.

"Yeah, the feeling is pretty mutual," I said, shifting my body as I felt his erection beneath me.

My movement made his grip on my body tighten.

"Cyn..." he nearly growled, and I moved again, more deliberately. "I should probably...get you back to your place...You probably still have to pack and—"

I cut off his words by kissing him again. When I pulled away, I grinned at him.

"What happened to wanting to elongate the moment?" I asked, causing his lips to form a smirk that was so damn sexy my nipples hardened.

"I was trying to be chivalrous," he admitted.

"And while I appreciate that," I said. "I'm not...I'm not ready for whatever this is to end."

"What would you like then?" he asked.

"I'd like to go back to *your* place," I told him. "Cause I've heard sex on the beach ain't really as great as all the movies and books make it out to be."

His eyes widened with my bluntness, but I felt his dick twitch beneath my ass. I let out a little yelp when he abruptly stood and helped me up.

"My place it is then," he said, and we rushed back to his car.

4

———

We pulled up to the Lillian Resort and Hotel and as soon as I stepped out of the car, I was greeted by a valet driver.

"Welcome back, Mr. Kn–"

I reached out and took his hand in mine, shaking it as I slid him my keys and a large bill. His grin widened at the sight of the cash in his hand, and I gave him a friendly nod before going around to the other side of the car to open the door for Cyn. Once I helped her out of the car, I gently placed my hand at the small of her back and guided her into the hotel.

We bypassed the regular elevators and went to the private one that would take me directly up to the suite I'd booked for my stay.

26

My grandmother had tried to persuade me to stay with her, insisting that I didn't need to waste money when she had a perfectly good room waiting for me.

Now, looking over at Cyn, I was glad that I'd politely declined her offer. Her scolding was worth it, I thought as I used my keycard to unlock access to the elevator.

The elevator doors closed and I looked over to find Cyn nervously fiddling with a bracelet around her wrist. I reached over and took her hand in mine, interlocking our fingers.

"Cyn...if you've changed your mind–"

"I haven't," she said quickly. "I haven't."

"Good," I said, pulling her towards me until our bodies were pressed against one another. I slid my free hand into her hair and tilted her head back and captured her mouth in a kiss.

She'd been straight with me about why she wanted to come here, so there was no point in wasting the little time together we had left.

I heard Cyn let out a little whimper as she opened her mouth, allowing me to deepen the kiss. The elevator pinged, alerting me that we'd made it to the penthouse and I bent down slightly to grab her thighs and lifted her into my arms.

She hooked her legs around my waist as I stumbled to the bedroom and when we made it to the room I headed straight for the bed.

I laid Cyn down on the mattress as I continued kissing her, moving from her mouth to her neck, where I sank my teeth into her soft skin just enough to make her squirm beneath me.

I inhaled deeply, committing her scent to my memory. Damn, she smelled so fucking amazing. I pushed her t-shirt up and ran my fingers against her stomach before planting a kiss there.

Wanting to see more of her...*needing* to see more of her, I sat up and brought her with me, lifted her shirt off of her head, tossing it to the floor and then unhooked her bra.

I palmed one of her breasts in my hand and she let out a hiss of breath when I sucked her tight nipple into my mouth.

She broke the connection when she yanked my shirt over my head, but once it was gone my mouth was on her body again; kissing, licking and nibbling.

I unsnapped the button of her shorts and pulled them, along with her panties, down her legs. Once they were off, I stood and looked down at her.

She was...fucking amazing.

And she was staring up at me with a look of hunger in her eyes that made me eager to get inside of her. So I quickly shed the rest of my clothes, grabbed a condom out of my wallet, and climbed back on top of her, crushing my mouth to hers as I slid two fingers between her thick folds.

Her hips lifted as I kept playing with her pussy, her juices coating my fingers.

"Rome," Cyn moaned into my ear.

I sat up again, opened the condom and covered myself, and then I grabbed Cyn's legs and spread them wide.

I slid inside of her, and...

"Shit..." I growled.

I got lost with every inch that I sank into her. My fingers dug into her thighs as I slowly moved in and out of her, damn near pulling out before diving even deeper than I was before.

I felt Cyn's fingers grab my locs and my dick seemed to grow even harder. I grabbed her wrists and locked them over her head with one hand and grabbed one of her legs and hooked it over my shoulder.

"Oh...oh...*oh!*" Cyn cried out as I continued pounding her body over and over.

Her legs began to tremble, and her moans grew louder and louder until she screamed my name.

I felt her clench around my dick and I let out a groan as I exploded.

I laid there for a moment to catch my breath and got up went to the bathroom to get rid of the condom and get cleaned up. I grabbed a towel, wet it with warm water and headed back to the room.

I found Cyn lying on the bed with one of her arms draped over her face.

"You good, gorgeous?" I asked as I got back into the bed.

"Better than good," she drawled, a soft moan escaping her lips when I began wiping between her legs with the towel.

The sound of her stomach growling filled the bedroom and she covered her face with her hands.

"And apparently hungry," I teased. I pulled her hands away from her face and leaned over to kiss her lips. "Don't fret, beautiful. I'm definitely gonna feed your fine ass."

She was going to need all of her strength for what I had in store for her for the rest of the night.

If I was only getting one night with this woman, I was damn sure gonna make it one neither of us never forgot.

"There aren't any utensils in here," I said, digging around in the bag that held the food Rome had picked up for us.

Rome looked up at me and smiled.

I'd dozed off shortly after Rome cleaned me up. I vaguely heard him say he'd be right back and I found myself being awaken by the scent of food, and Rome's lips on my shoulder. I also noticed when he'd dropped a new box of unopened condoms on the bedside table.

"You mean you've been in Trinidad all this time and haven't had doubles?" he asked.

I shook my head. "Jaclyn's ass has been dragging us to every fast food joint she could find. I kept telling her I can eat that shit back at home and we should try new things. But there was no getting her to try anything new, except for the drinks."

Rome laughed and shook his head.

"I guess it's a good thing the golden arches is global."

"That's *highly* debatable," I said, rolling my eyes. I inhaled deeply and leaned forward. "This smells really good."

"It tastes even better," Rome said, unwrapping one of the wax papers that held the food. He passed it to me and then opened another one.

"Sooo...what exactly *is* doubles?" I asked, looking down at the food

"It's curried chickpeas called channa," Rome explained. "And it's sandwiched between a spicy fried dough called bara."

"Oh cool," I said, reaching down to pick it up when Rome stopped me.

"You gotta eat doubles like a true Trini, gorgeous."

"And how do you eat doubles like a true Trini?"

"There's really nothing to it," he said, as he picked up one of the pieces of bread. "You just use the bara to scoop up the channa and..." He took a big bite and I just sat there, staring as he chewed his food.

It made no fucking sense for a man to look that damn sexy just eating. Rome looked up at me and grinned, tilting his head towards my lap. "You should try it before it gets cold."

"Oh...yeah..."

I did as he'd showed me and took a big bite of my food.

"Oh..." I said over a mouthful of food. "This is..."

I didn't speak, *couldn't* speak. All I could do was take

another bite, not giving a damn that I had food running down the corners of my mouth.

"Here."

I looked up and saw Rome was holding a glass bottle of a red drink out to me. I took it from him and read the label. "Solo," I said, before taking a sip. "Wow."

"We could never have doubles and not have Solo Soda," Rome said.

"I see why. It's a great combo."

I finished my doubles and Rome must have sensed that I was hoping for more, because he reached into the bag, pulled out another one and handed it to me. I immediately snatched it from his hands and quickly opened it up and devoured it.

"That was so delicious," I said, once I was finished eating. "I kinda wanna fight Jaclyn for damn near making me miss out on that."

"Coming to Trinidad and not trying doubles is almost an insult."

"Well, thank you," I said, gathering the trash up from the bed. I threw it away and then headed for the bathroom.

I relieved myself, washed my hands and then grabbed the travel-sized mouthwash off of the counter and took a small swig. After swishing it around and spitting it out, I headed back to the bedroom, where I found Rome sitting up, his back against the headboard with his eyes closed.

I stood there staring at him, my gaze transfixed on the slow, even rise and fall of his broad chest. His eyes fluttered open just as I was licking my lips and he gave me a mesmeric grin.

"Still hungry?" he asked, as he stretched his arms over his head.

"Not exactly," I replied.

He put his hands behind his head and his eyes heatedly roamed my body from head to toe.

"What...exactly are you then?"

Knowing I could show him way better than I could tell him, I undid the sash of the robe he'd given me to wear and let it fall to the ground.

I sauntered over to the bed and then crawled my way over to Rome, until I was in his lap, my mouth on his.

He wasted no time taking control of the kiss, and I blindly reached for the box of condoms on the drawer. We quickly tore it open, grabbed several packages, and after he ripped one open and covered himself, he took me by the hips and guided me down onto his massive erection.

I planted my hands on his shoulders, giving myself leverage as I moved up and down on him. Every time I hit the base of his shaft, I'd roll my hips and he'd let out a grunt and he met my move with a hard upward pump, nearly driving me insane.

His hand wrapped around my neck and he squeezed with just enough force to turn me on, but at the same time, I felt a gentleness in his touch as well.

His hand moved from my neck to my breast, and he rolled my nipple between his fingertips before pulling it into his mouth, causing my back to bow.

My skin began to tingle and I began bouncing wildly on his dick.

Rome suddenly sat up on his knees and spun us around on the bed, pressing my back against the headboard. I wrapped my legs around his waist, relishing in every single furious thrust, until I came unglued, screaming at the top of my lungs.

I was no screamer.

But with Rome...apparently he was the exception.

"Cyn," he gritted out and I opened my eyes to find him staring at me. That same intensity that was too much for me to handle was in his eyes and I tried to look away. But Rome grabbed my face with his hand, forcing me to look at him.

And then he kissed me.

A soul-stirring, toe-curling, all-consuming kiss.

And then I came again.

———

"What time is it?"

The sound of Rome's groggy voice caused me to look over my shoulder. I glanced at the clock on the nightstand table and then back at Rome. "Almost midnight," I said as I finished putting on my shoes.

He sat up and noticed that I was dressed.

"You have to go." He wasn't asking. He knew. Our time together had come to an end.

"Yeah," I said. "My flight is pretty early."

"Gimme a few minutes to get dressed and I'll drive you home," he said, standing up.

"You don't have to do that," I said. "I can call a cab."

"Cyn, it's dangerous to be out at this time of night," Rome said, sitting up. "I wouldn't feel right letting you go out there alone."

"I'll be *fine*," I insisted.

We stood there, staring at each other for several moments and just when I thought he was going to continue arguing the subject, he shut his eyes and blew out a breath.

"Okay," he conceded. He grabbed his phone. "But *no* cabs. I have a car service on standby. You can use that instead."

Before I could respond he'd put his phone to his ear and was ordering a car to take me back to my rental. He hung up and grabbed his pants off the floor.

"I'll walk you to the lobby," he said, as he started getting dressed.

I nodded, figuring I may as well extend these last few moments with him as much as I could.

After he was done putting on the rest of his clothes, we headed for the elevator.

It was an awkward silence that floated between us. I turned and opened my mouth to speak – not completely sure what to say – but Rome cupped my face and dropped his mouth over mine.

I swallowed the nonsensical lump that had formed in my throat and melted into the bittersweet kiss.

I felt the goodbye in the tender way he greedily nibbled on my bottom lip.

The elevator doors opened and we slowly parted. Rome took my hand in his as we walked through the lobby.

The car Rome had ordered was already waiting for me when we got outside.

"I got it," Rome said to the driver as he opened the back door for me. "Make sure she gets to her destination. Safely."

The driver nodded and hurried around to the other side of the car, got in and started it.

I turned to Rome and smiled.

He reached up and tucked a strand of hair behind my ear.

"You were quite an unexpected, but fascinating surprise," Rome said, his fingers caressing my jaw.

"So were you," I replied. I rose up on my toes, gave Rome one last kiss and then got into the town car. Rome shut the door and the chauffeur began to drive away.

"Where to, Miss?" he asked as we left the hotel.

I gave him the address and sank into the plush back seat. In no time, we were pulling up to the house.

The chauffeur got out and opened my door for me.

"Thank you," I said and he nodded. I hurried up the walkway, unlocked the door and quietly slipped into the house so I wouldn't wake Jaclyn and Octavia.

But they were wide awake sitting on the couch.

Jaclyn gave me a once over and her mouth spread into a wide grin.

"Oh he *really* dicked you down, girl!"

I shook my head and headed for my room as Jaclyn and Octavia fell into a fit of laughter.

"Good*night!*" I said before slamming the door, a smirk on my face as I thought about Rome.

He truly had been an unexpected, yet *fascinating* surprise.

And it had been the perfect way to bring my vacation to an end.

5

I'd just come out of the bathroom and dumped my toiletry bag into my suitcase when I heard my cell phone ring. I grabbed my phone off of the nightstand drawer and smiled at the name flashing across the screen. I pressed the answer button and put the phone on speaker as I continued packing.

"Izzy, what's up?"

"Roman!" Isabella said brightly. "How's my favorite cousin?"

I stopped packing and looked down at my phone.

"Damn, you're laying it on thick right out the gate. What do you want?"

"Why do I have to want something?" she argued. "Can't I just be calling to see how you're doing?"

"Iz..." I chuckled. "Just spit it out."

"Fine. I'm working on my spring and summer lines, which include my latest bridal wear..."

"Great," I said, leaning down to pick up a pair of shoes. A glimmer of something under the bed caught my eye, and I got down on my knees and reached under the bed to grab whatever it was.

"And it would be amazing if my world-renowned photographer cousin could capture the collection for me."

I looked down at the small silver charm in the shape of a heeled shoe, and instantly realized...

It belonged to Cynthia.

I remembered the charm bracelet that she'd been wearing around her wrist. This particular charm had obviously fallen off at some point during the night when we'd...

Damn...I thought to myself as I sat down on the bed.

Instantly, memories of our time together – specifically in the bed I was sitting on – came flooding back to the forefront of my mind.

The way she smelled.

The way her skin felt beneath my fingers.

The way her face looked as she came–

"Roman? Rome, are you still there?"

I blinked, and looked over at my phone, realizing that I'd completely forgotten that I'd been on the phone with Izzy.

"Uh, yeah. Photoshoot. Fashion line. Whatever you need, cuz. You know I got you."

"Thank you!" she squealed. "I'm still getting everything together, we're still going back and forth with our model and when she'll be available. We want her to come to Sweet Rapids and she won't be available for a few weeks."

"Who's the model?" I absently asked, still staring at the charm.

This time it was Izzy who took a long time to respond.

Finally, she mumbled, "Priscilla Tremaine." *That* shit caused me to snap out of my Cyn-induced trance.

"Priscilla?!" I groaned.

"Look..." Izzy started. "I *know* you and Priscilla have...history."

"Don't say it like that, Iz," I grumbled.

"Say it like what?"

"Like it was more than what it was."

"So enlighten me, dear cousin. What exactly did happen between you and Priscilla ?"

"Not a fucking thing," I explained. "I did a few of her shoots a few years ago. We went out for drinks after a shoot once, to celebrate. When she tried to get at me, you know beyond business, I shut that shit down immediately and let her know I wasn't interested in her in that way."

Unfortunately, I'd gotten photographed with her that night, and because of the way Priscilla had been pushing up on me, it made us look like more than what we actually were. The gossip columns ran wild with assumptions about our 'relationship', and rather than correct them, Priscilla − who I discovered enjoyed bending the truth to her benefit − fed into the fodder of it all.

I hadn't worked with her since then, but I'd heard rumors that Priscilla had grown to be a difficult client to work with.

"Iz...I don't know−" I sighed.

"Rome, *please*," Izzy begged.

I should have reneged as soon as I found out that Priscilla Tremaine would be the model I'd be shooting, or at least offered some better options to Izzy. But against my better judgment I found myself saying, "Hit me up when all the details for the shoot are finalized."

"Thank you!" she said again. "Oh! How was Carnival?"

Once again that made me think of Cyn, and I couldn't help but smile.

"It was amazing."

"I'm sure it was. Ivy's been a few times..."

We chatted for a few more minutes before getting off the phone, agreeing to link up when I got back home to Nevada.

I hung up the phone and turned my attention back to the charm in my hand. Cyn was probably long gone back to...wherever it was she was from.

We hadn't discussed that.

We also hadn't given our last names to one another, I suddenly realized once I picked up my phone again to try to search for her online.

"Shit..." I swore, shaking my head.

I stood, and tucked the charm away in my suitcase, wondering if Cyn had discovered that she'd lost it yet and how she would react once she did.

I cried the entire flight home.

And then I cried for a good two or three more days after.

My bracelet was the last gift my father had given me, and that heel charm represented the first daddy/daughter dance he'd taken me to.

It was my own damn fault. I knew the charm was loose and I should have taken it to get fixed ages ago. But I never had the time because—

"Cyn!"

I cleaned up my face and left the bathroom to look for Priscilla. I found her in the living room, sitting on the couch with Maggie, her Yorkshire terrier, holding the drink I'd run out to get her, with an annoyed look on her face.

Clearing my throat, I asked, "What's up, Priscilla?"

"This is the wrong drink," she griped, slamming it down on the coffee table.

"Sorry," I mumbled as I picked up the drink.

She tilted her head to the side and studied me as she stroked Maggie's back.

"You've been...off ever since you got back from your little girl's trip. First you forget about my conference call with Lorenzo in Milan. Now this. I'm gonna need you to get your shit together. Or I can call mother–"

"That's not necessary, Priscilla."

I turned on my heels and walked off, but her words stopped me.

"I've got a shoot coming up in a couple weeks, for Izzy Noble-Hill's fashion line. Get with Lily to get all the details so you can book our travel arrangements."

I nodded and kept walking, scooping up her mail to sort out later on.

I went to the room that was designated as my office and checked my planner. I still had a handful of errands to run today, including go to the grocery store, drop Maggie off at the groomers and go to the dry cleaners and pick up a dress for an event Priscilla would be attending this weekend.

That last errand reminded me that I still needed to respond to the other invites Priscilla had received. I spent the next hour sifting through the invitations with Priscilla, checking her calendar and sending out acceptances to the ones she wanted to go to and her schedule allowed for her to attend; and then declining the ones she was either unavailable to attend or just flat out didn't want to go to.

Once we were finished, I headed back to the office.

Lily, who was sitting at her desk, turned and gave me a sympathetic smile. She knew about me losing my charm. She placed a hand on my arm and gave it a supportive squeeze.

"I've taken care of all the travel arrangements for the two of you for your trip to Sweet Rapids."

"Thank you so much, Lily."

Priscilla may not have trusted Lily in her role as an executive assistant yet, but I did.

"Why don't you take off early?" Lily suggested. "Go home. I'll cover for you."

Shaking my head, I quickly declined. "I couldn't. Priscilla would have a fit."

"And she'd get over it," Lily insisted. "I'm not afraid of Priscilla."

No matter how much of a bitch Priscilla was towards her, no matter what she threw at her – literally once or twice – Lily handled it all with grace and the patience of a saint.

She was made for this job and would do well if I decided to leave.

When I decided to leave.

Jaclyn and Octavia were right, I couldn't keep working for Priscilla.

I had a fucking master's degree going to waste all because I felt like I owed it to Priscilla and my stepmother to stay.

After my father died, and no will was found, everything – including my father's company – went to Linda. At one point, I found myself on the verge of having to drop out of college, because even with student loans, it wasn't enough to help me continue. But I felt like I *had* to finish college. So I went to Linda and *begged* for help, which, surprisingly, she agreed to do. Unsurprisingly, there were strings attached.

Well...just one string.

Priscilla.

She'd been modeling since she was a kid, in fact it's how our parents first met. Linda had been on the hunt to find Priscilla a new modeling agency to work with and ended up signing a contract with Tremaine Modeling Agency – my father's company.

It didn't take long for my father to become smitten with Linda, and Priscilla. A year after they met, Linda and my dad were married and he adopted Priscilla (who'd never known her birth father).

In my mind, I thought we'd be the perfect little family, but I was horribly wrong.

Linda was always cold towards me, showing just enough affection in my father's presence to make him think she was a doting stepmother to his daughter.

But Priscilla...

Priscilla had *always* been awful to me. No matter what I did to please her, she always complained.

Not much had changed once we were adults and I ended up as her executive assistant. It was Linda's caveat to the money I needed in order to continue going to college.

Looking back, I don't know how the hell I managed it. Juggling Priscilla's entire life *and* earning my degrees, but I did it.

I missed both my undergrad and master's graduations, because even though I'd let Priscilla know months in advance, when the time came around, there was always something that she needed me to do or someplace she needed me to go that she felt was more important.

I should have quit back then, but I stayed on, and I saved my money.

I had more than enough money to quit and live comfortably for a while. Until I could find a job that I actually enjoyed.

*Whatever the hell that is...*I thought to myself.

I looked at my sketchbook on my desk and then back at Lily.

"If you need me—"

"I'll call. Go!"

I gave Lily a grateful smile, snatched up my sketchbook and took off, thankful when I didn't have a run-in with Priscilla on my way out.

6

———————

Roman

"Give these a try."

I looked up as my brother Remington, placed a flight of beers down on the table in front of me and my other brother, Ramsey.

I'd driven down to Remi's place in Sweet Rapids to kick it with him and Ram. It was the first time we'd all been able to link up since I'd gotten back from Trinidad.

"So," Ram started as he picked up one of the craft beers Remi had created. "How's Ajee?"

"She told me to tell you that you'd know your damn selves if you actually came to see her," I said, referring to our grandmother. "But it just reinforced why I'm the favorite grandson."

Remi rolled his eyes and took a sip of the beer. "Too hoppy."

Ram and I both took a sip of the same beer and shrugged. It tasted fine to us, but Remi was the expert, so we didn't argue. We spent the next hour trying the rest of the beers, Remi seeming to find something wrong with every single one of them, while Ram and I just enjoyed each one.

Remington had been on edge ever since he'd put the wheels in motion to open up his own brewery in Sweet Rapids. He wanted just the right flavors for Knight Brewery, especially since whatever would become his signature beer would be the one that he would end up pitching to be served in our cousin Ian's restaurants.

"Five star restaurants need a five star beer," he told us over and over again.

"You bring your camera?" Ramsey asked, later on when we were sitting on the couch in front of the TV watching a game and eating wings we'd ordered to go along with all of Remi's beers.

"Of course," I said.

"Let's see those Carnival pictures then!" he said.

"Pull them up on the TV," Remi said and I nodded, sliding my SD card into a jump drive. I plugged the drive into a slot on the back of the TV and Remi grabbed the remote to go to the input channel that would bring up the pics.

They started scrolling through the photos, while I went to the kitchen to get more wings.

"These are great, Rome," Remi said. "You really captured the spirit of Carnival."

"Thanks, man."

When I heard Ramsey shout, "Goddamn!" I knew from his exclamation that they were looking at Cyn's pics.

I looked up at the TV and saw her, in her costume, arms in the air, a look of pure ecstasy on her face.

From just staring at her picture, I could suddenly feel the warmth of the island, smell the street food, hear the music.

And then Remi clicked to another picture of Cyn looking directly at the camera and it was as if she was right there in the living room, tempting me all over again.

"Yo! Earth to Rome!"

I blinked and looked over at the couch to find both of my brothers staring at me curiously.

"What did you say?" I asked.

Ram narrowed his gaze at me and then looked over at Remi.

"He hooked up with her," they said in tandem.

I shook my head, and loaded my plate up with more food, before heading back to the couch.

I sat down and looked up to find my brothers still staring at me.

"*What*?!" I yelled.

"So you just not gone tell us shit?" Remi asked, a smirk on his face.

"Nope," I said, taking a huge bite out of one of the wings.

"Seriously?" Ram asked.

"Seriously," I said over a mouthful of food. "Mind ya damn business."

"She must've had your nose *wide* the fuck open if you don't even want to talk about it," Remi said, as he kept clicking through the photos of Cyn.

"Shit, look at her!" Ram said, whistling.

I stood again, went to the TV and snatched my SD card out and shoved it into my pocket.

I went and sat back down and Ram said, "Since you don't wanna talk about the baddie you got with in Trinidad, how 'bout we discuss you having to work with Priscilla again soon."

"Nothing to discuss," I said. "Izzy chose her to be the face of her upcoming fashion line and asked me to do the photos."

"You're seriously not buggin' about havin' to work with that crazy woman?" Remi asked.

"I can handle Priscilla," I said, taking a sip of one of the few beers that had passed this round of Remi's inspection. "Either of you bozos heard from Mom?"

Ever since my aunt Irene had turned over their family business, Noble Naturals to my cousins – with Isaiah at the helm – she and my mother, Ruby, had been enjoying their days of retirement to the fullest, traveling all over the world. It wasn't uncommon for us to get a text at a moment's notice from our mom telling us she and Aunt Irene were jetting off and adding another stamp to their passport.

But after raising all of us, they more than deserved.

"Nah," Remi said. "But I talked to Ian today and he said he heard from Aunt Irene. He said they're having a good time on their European cruise. They're in Spain."

I knew as much from the pictures my mother had posted on social media.

"I'm sure she'll be calling us soon," I said. She never went too long without reaching out to us.

I hung out with my brothers for a few more hours before heading back to my condo in Reno. I headed straight for my bedroom where I stripped down out of my clothes, intent on heading for the shower. The sound of something clanging on the floor caught my attention and I realized it was the SD jump drive that held the pictures of Cynthia on it. I picked it up off of the floor and put it on my dresser before continuing on towards the shower.

But now Cyn was once again on my mind.

For some reason there'd been this...unspoken agreement that whatever happened between us in Trinidad was going to stay in Trinidad; but looking back on things now, I regretted the decision more and more that I didn't get any contact information from her to keep in touch.

Realizing there was no point in dwelling on what could have been, I stepped into the shower, got cleaned up and then headed for bed to turn in for the night. I was meeting up with Izzy in the morning to go over plans for the upcoming shoot with Priscilla.

She was arriving in a week and I needed to prepare myself for whatever bullshit I knew she had up her sleeve.

"Let me help you with those bags, Miss Tremaine."

I gave the flight attendant a grateful smile as he grabbed two of the travel bags I'd been trying to get up the stairs of the private plane after Priscilla had boarded. The only bag she'd carried was the dog purse that was holding Maggie inside.

"Thank you," I said once we were on the plane and had gotten the luggage stowed away.

"Not a problem," he said, as he cut an annoyed eye in Priscilla's direction. When he brought his gaze back to me, his countenance was much more friendly. "The pilot says skies are clear and we should be taking off on time. The flight to Reno is just over six hours."

I nodded and turned to make my way to the back of the plane when Priscilla grunted and handed me Maggie.

"Sweet Rapids!" she spat out. "I don't know why we have to meet them *there*."

"That *is* where Izzy's fashion house is, Priscilla," I reminded her.

"Still, we could have at least stayed in Reno…" she pouted, and I continued towards the back of the plane with Maggie in tow. Priscilla's voice perked up when she sighed, "The *one* good thing about this shoot is I'll get to work with Roman again. He did my first shoot in Paris. We kind of had a thing going on back then…"

Already tuning out Priscilla – it was the only way I was gonna get through a six and a half hour flight with her ass – I pulled my sketchbook out, along with my pencils and flipped to my latest work in progress. I tucked my earbuds into my ears, cranked up my music and started drawing.

I paused for a moment when I remembered the name of the photographer that Priscilla had mentioned.

Roman…

Of course it made me think of Rome.

I pretty much always have a camera with me…

My eyes narrowed wondering what the odds were that.

I shook my head in denial.

"There's no way," I said under my breath, as I went back to work.

The flight was, thankfully, uneventful and we landed in Reno in the late afternoon. After the thirty minute drive to Sweet Rapids we arrived at the rental house that Isabella Noble had comped us for our stay for the duration of our trip.

"Wow," I said, pulling into the circular driveway.

Izzy hadn't skimped on the accommodations, I thought as I got out of the car looking at the gorgeous Mediterranean-style home we'd be staying in for the next week.

"It'll do," Priscilla grumbled as she flounced up the walkway with Maggie to the front door. She stopped and dramatically pivoted on her heels. "*Cynthia!*"

I blinked and looked over at her and she scoffed and rolled her eyes. "The door," she barked.

I slammed the car door and hurried to the front door and punched in the code to the lockbox to get the keys to the house out.

We went inside and I was stunned by the spacious two-story home with floor to ceiling windows that showed off a stunning view of the lake the house sat on as well as the mountains in the distance.

I was on my way to get a closer look at the view when Priscilla thrusted Maggie's carrier into my arms.

"I'm going to find a suitable room upstairs and decompress."

That meant I needed to make myself scarce for the next several hours.

I watched Priscilla head for the stairs and once a bedroom door slammed, effectively dismissing me, I looked down at Maggie.

"What do you say, girl? Wanna go explore Sweet Rapids?"

Maggie gave me an affirmative bark and I took her out of her carrier and clipped her leash to her collar and led her back outside to the car.

I'd done a bit of research on the town and found a bunch of articles on Sweet Rapids, specifically the historic district in the downtown area, and how it had been revitalized over the last decade. A lot of the revitalization had been under the influence of Isaac Noble, the late patriarch of the Noble family.

I figured that area of the city was as good a place as any to start my little adventure with Maggie; so I plugged in Main Street in the GPS and took off.

It was a short drive and once I found a parking spot, I grabbed Maggie and got out of the car. I sat her down on the ground and we took off.

We took our time strolling down the sidewalk, smiling at the few people that we occasionally passed.

I stopped in front of a vacant building that had a 'coming soon' sign in the window.

"Knight Brewery," I mused before moving on down the sidewalk. I kept walking, looking through all of the store front windows, taking a mental note of all the places I wanted to visit when I didn't have Maggie with me.

There was a gallery that had some amazing pottery on display in the window.

And across the street was a bakery that had the most amazing smelling baked goods.

There was also a yoga studio that offered a variety of different classes including heated yoga and aerial yoga.

I was also happy to see that there was a juice bar, something I'm sure Priscilla would approve of.

Speaking of Priscilla...

At the distinct ringtone from my phone, I knew my free time with Maggie had come to an end.

"Yes, Priscilla ?"

"Where are you?"

"You said you needed time to decompress so I took Maggie on a walk."

"Well, since you're out, I'm hungry."

"I'll see what I can find," I said, and hung up.

"I'm thinking of putting the bar over here..."

I nodded at Remi's idea as we walked around the space he'd bought for the brewery. It was in a good location in the historic district of Downtown Sweet Rapids. And just a few doors down from my photography studio.

I was listening to Remi when out of the corner of my eye, I caught the glimpse of a woman walking by.

A woman that looked a hell of a lot like Cyn.

I rushed over to the window, but by the time I got there, the woman was gone.

"Rome? You okay?" Remi asked, coming to stand next to me by the window.

"Huh? Oh, yeah I'm cool," I said, shaking my head. "Just thought I saw someone..."

It was bad enough that she showed up in my dreams all the time; now my eyes were clearly playing tricks on me while I was awake, making me think I'd just seen a woman I'd spent one night with weeks ago in Sweet Rapids of all places.

"There's no way..." I murmured, still looking out the window.

"No way what?" Remi asked, confused.

"Nothing," I said, finally turning away from the window. "Come on, show me the rest of your plans."

7

———

I'd just settle down for the evening, with Maggie fast asleep near my feet, when my tablet began ringing, alerting me of a video chat call.

I smiled and picked up my tablet.

"Faye!" I gushed when my godmother's face popped up on the screen. "I was just thinking about you."

Faye gave me a warm smile. "And what about me were you thinking, Cynthia my love?"

"About how I need to come see you since I'm in your neck of the woods."

"Get out of town!" she shouted.

"Well if I did, you wouldn't get to see me," I teased.

Faye Avery had been my mother's best friend since

53

childhood. They were practically sisters minus the same DNA. So when my mother passed away when I was seven, she'd taken the loss hard. She stepped in and helped take care of me, until my father met and married Linda.

Faye and Linda absolutely did not get along.

Faye couldn't stand Linda because she'd always felt that the only thing about my father that she was interested in was his money. And when Linda accused Faye of using me to get closer to her dead best friend's husband...let's just say Faye didn't take too kindly to that.

So Faye fell back.

But her presence was always felt. Even with the distance between us, Faye was always there for me, making sure she was available whenever I needed a shoulder to cry on.

"Where are you?" Faye asked.

"I'm in a town called Sweet Rapids."

"Oh where Noble Naturals is located!" she said. "It's beautiful out there."

"It really is. Priscilla has a shoot with Izzy Noble-Hill actually. For her fashion line."

"Priscilla," Faye said with a roll of her eyes. "How is the little brat?"

"She's...Priscilla," I said with a shrug. "We'll be here for a few days, so I'm gonna find time to come out and see you."

"You better," Faye demanded. "It's been so long."

"It has."

"Oh! I haven't talked to you since you got back from your trip to Trinidad. How was it?"

"It was amazing," I replied. "Carnival was great. Jaclyn and Octavia convinced me to wear one of those costumes to the parade."

"The ones that have all of your goodies hanging out?! *You* wore one of those?" Faye gasped.

"Yep," I nodded, with a grin. "Hold on, let me send you some pics."

I went to the photo album app and selected a few pics that Octavia had taken of me and sent them to Faye.

"Damn!" I heard her exclaim as she looked at the pics. "You were *working it*, baby girl. I bet you had to beat all them fine island men off with a stick."

My cheeks heated at the thought of Rome, and when I simply responded with a shy laugh, Faye's eyebrows perked up.

"You met someone, didn't you?"

"It was nothing, Faye."

"Oh...it was something, baby girl. Tell me all about him."

"There's not much to tell," I said. "We met during the parade, shared a dance. Ran into each other again the next day at a cafe. We talked, spent the day...and night together and then I left. And that was the end of it."

"Seems like he had quite the effect on you even in the short amount of time you spent together," Faye prodded.

"Doesn't matter," I huffed. "It wasn't meant to be more than that one night. We didn't exchange last names, contact information...nothing."

We talked for a little while longer, before hanging up so I could get some rest.

Our call time to the shoot at the studio, Knight Photography, was seven in the morning so Priscilla could get her hair and makeup done and I needed all the rest I could get.

We arrived at the studio the next morning and were greeted by Izzy Noble-Hill herself.

She gave us a warm welcome and introduced Priscilla to the head of the style team and then Priscilla was whisked off to get ready for the shoot.

"Mrs. Noble-Hill," I said, once Priscilla was gone.

She waved a hand at me. "That is such a mouthful. Please, just call me Izzy."

I nodded and lowered my voice. "I just wanted to tell you... I'm a *huge* fan of your work. I shop at your New York store all of the time."

"Thank you! You should check out my shop here while you're in town," she said with a playful wink.

"Oh, I *definitely* am," I assured her.

She looked over her shoulder and a smile spread across her face. "Oh! I'd like you to meet the photographer, who also happens to be my cousin, Roman Knight. Roman! I'd like you to meet...I'm sorry, I didn't catch your name."

I spun around and froze.

He looked up from the camera he'd been working with in his hands and his eyes grew wide.

"*Cyn*?!" he whispered. He looked around confused, but excited. "Wh–what are you doing here?"

"You two know each other?" Izzy asked, looking from Rome back to me.

I couldn't speak, couldn't move... until he moved towards me, his arms outstretched as if he wanted to pull me into a hug.

And then I caught Priscilla curiously staring at us.

I quickly took a step back and grabbed his hand and shook it.

"I'm Cynthia...Priscilla's personal assistant."

"You're...what?"

"I'd...better go see how things are going with Priscilla," Izzy said, leaving me alone with Rome.

"That *was* you I saw yesterday," he said, in awe. "In town across the street. I thought I was trippin', but..." His gaze took me in from head to toe. "This must be some kind of kismet shit or something. How are you?"

"I–"

"Roman!" I looked up and saw Priscilla heading for us. She brushed past me, and threw her arms around Roman's neck, aiming her mouth for his and he quickly dodged it.

"Priscilla," he said in an annoyed tone.

"That's how you greet me...after all this time?"

That's when it hit me.

Like a fucking punch in the gut.

This was who Priscilla had been talking about all this time.

The Roman she'd had a thing with...was also the Rome that I'd...

"Excuse me," I said, backing away, feeling sick to my stomach.

"Cynthia," Izzy caught up with me, concern etched on her face. "Are you okay?"

"Where's your restroom?" I asked.

Izzy pointed me in the right direction and I took off. When I got to the restroom, I rushed to a stall and locked myself inside.

I pressed my back against the stall door, my chest heaving as I tried to catch my breath. I leaned forward, planting my hands on my knees as I swallowed a scream.

I covered my mouth and squeezed my eyes shut, no longer able to hold back the hot tears that streamed down my face.

I stayed there for several minutes, just allowing myself this moment to feel...whatever the hell it was I was feeling.

Once I regained my composure, I left the stall, went to the mirror, washed my face and reminded myself that I was here to do my job.

I just couldn't wait until this particular assignment was over so I could get the fuck out of here.

Roman

She was avoiding me.

Ever since our awkward reunion the other day – which had been interrupted by Priscilla's overdramatic ass – Cynthia had done everything in her power to put distance between us.

Our reactions to seeing each other again had been vastly different.

While I'd been excited – so much so that I'd almost dropped my camera when I looked up and saw her face – Cyn had been quite the opposite.

I tried to argue that maybe she was just trying to keep things professional since she was Priscilla's personal assistant, but the few times I managed to catch her staring at me, her eyes were...cold as hell.

If looks could kill, man...

I watched as Cyn brought Priscilla a sparkling water, with a straw in it.

Cyn looked...different.

That wild beautiful hair that I hadn't been able to keep my hands out of was slicked back into a tight bun. Her outfit was a simple T-shirt, jeans and running shoes.

But it wasn't her hair or clothes, it was her entire demeanor that was a stark contrast from the woman I'd met while in Trinidad.

It reminded me of what she'd said to me on the beach.

My job is not to be seen.

Something about seeing her like this...a mere shadow of the woman that I'd met, fucked with my head.

But there wasn't anything I could do about it at the moment.

"Alright," I shouted. "We've only got a few hours of good sun left."

We were on location for this round of photos. Izzy wanted some shots out in nature.

Unfortunately, Priscilla wasn't exactly one with nature.

She'd been complaining about one thing or another the entire time we'd been out here.

"Roman," she whined. "Can't we do this back at the studio and you work your computer magic or whatever and just make it *look* like I was in the mountains?"

"It's more authentic this way, Priscilla," I said, holding my camera up. "Place your hand on your hip and rotate your upper body. Tilt your head..."

I continued directing her, snapping photo after photo. When I felt like I had enough, I wrapped for the afternoon. We were scheduled to meet up again the next day at another location.

I swallowed a groan when I saw Priscilla heading in my direction.

"Do you have any plans tonight?" she purred, gliding a finger over my arm. "I figured we could...catch up."

I looked past Priscilla and noticed Cyn watching us.

"Sorry," I said, pulling my arm away from Priscilla. "Can't."

"Fine," she pouted. She turned and headed for the SUV waiting to drive her back down the mountain. "*Cyn!* Let's go!"

Cyn refused to look my way as she brushed past me to get to the SUV.

"Cynthia, I need to talk to you."

She stopped for a moment and turned to look at me, her eyes filled with hurt.

"Unless it has something to do with Priscilla and the shoot,

I don't think we have anything to talk about, Mr. Knight," she said, her voice quiet as she averted her gaze from me.

And then she turned around again and headed for the SUV.

I watched as she got in and the vehicle drove away.

8

I walked out of my office at the studio and right into Cyn. She stumbled back and I reached out and grabbed her arms to keep her from falling and dropping the tray of fruit she was carrying.

"Damn," I said. "I'm sorry about that."

"It's fine," she said, trying to step around me. "Excuse me, I've gotta get this to Priscilla."

"Before you do that," I said. "Can you come in here for a moment? I have something I think might belong to you."

"Oh...I...okay," she said, looking over her shoulder before following me into the office.

I went to my desk, opened the top drawer and grabbed the charm.

I went to stand in front of her and held it up, watching as her eyes rounded in shock.

"You...you found it!" she gasped, putting the tray down on my desk. Her fingers trembled as she lifted her hand to take the charm.

She gazed down at it in the palm of her hand as tears began to drip down her face.

"Hey..." I said gently, reaching out to touch her shoulder. "Are you okay?"

She opened her mouth to speak and the only thing that came out was a strangled cry.

"I'm sorry," she said, waving at me and trying to take a step back, but I tightened my grip on her shoulder and pulled her into my arms.

My embrace seemed to open a floodgate and Cyn's sobs filled my office. I kicked my office door closed so no one walking by would see, and held her tighter, rubbing her back and letting her get it all out.

After a few minutes, she pulled away and looked up at me.

"You have no idea how much this means to me. This was part of the last gift my father gave to me before he died. Thank you, Rome."

"You're welcome." As she wiped her face with the back of her hand I took a chance and asked, "Since you're finally talking to me, you wanna tell me what it is that I did that's had you so upset with me?"

She looked up at me again for a moment and then looked away.

"Priscilla?" she said quietly.

"Priscilla?" I repeated confused. "What does Priscilla have to do with..."

That's when it clicked.

And Cyn noticed. "Yeah," she said, nodding her head,

once again looking everywhere but at me. "Priscilla hasn't stopped talking about the two of you."

"What has she been saying about the two of us?" I asked, quickly growing agitated.

"She's just been talking about how she couldn't wait to reconnect with you and how the two of you were...a thing."

"Priscilla's a goddamn liar."

Cyn's head whipped up at my words.

"Let me guess," I said, exasperated. "Priscilla's been running her mouth about us. You looked me up online and saw that stupid ass picture of the two of us and assumed everything she said was true."

Cyn nodded, and I ran a frustrated hand through my locs.

"There has *never* been anything between Priscilla and me beyond business. She's tried, but I've always made it clear to her that I'm not interested."

Cyn's mouth fell open.

"The two of you have never–"

"*Hell no*. Priscilla isn't my type." I took a step closer to her. "I prefer someone with much more...substance."

"I..." She placed her hand on her forehead, and she scrunched her nose. "I've been trippin'."

"Yeah...but all things considered...You seem to have known Priscilla much longer than you've known me, and–"

"That is *exactly* the point. I *know* Priscilla. And I should have known better than to believe her bullshit," she said. She looked up at me, remorse in her eyes. "I'm sorry, Rome. I should have just come to you and asked."

"Yeah. You should have. But it's all good," I said, reaching out to take her hand in mine. "You can make it up to me by letting me buy you a drink later tonight."

"Oh...Rome, I'd love to, but...Priscilla–"

"Can handle you being gone for a few hours," I prodded. "Do you have your phone on you?"

"Of course," she said, reaching into her back pocket. When she held it up, I took it from her, then handed it back a second later.

"It's locked."

"Oh!" she said, holding it up to her face to unlock it and then handed it back to me. "What are you doing?"

"What I should have done in Trinidad," I said, navigating to her contacts. "Here's my number. Text me later, and we'll figure out when to get you away from 'her majesty'."

I handed her back her phone, my fingers brushing hers in the process and I knew she felt the same thing I felt.

That spark we'd had when we'd first met in Trinidad was still there.

"Okay," she said, quietly. "I *really* need to get back to Priscilla. She's probably on the verge of a meltdown."

"We can't have that," I said, grinning down at her.

"No, we can't," Cyn said.

Neither of us made a move to leave though, we just continued staring at each other.

Until I finally said, "Fuck it," and palmed her face as I crushed my lips against hers.

Cyn let out a little whimper before her mouth opened and our tongues tangled with one another.

I tore my mouth away from hers and took a step back, the both of us, breathing heavily.

"Now I really *really* have to go," Cyn said, her cheeks flushed.

"That's probably a good idea," I said, shoving my hands into my pockets to adjust my pants.

Cyn's eyes zeroed in on my growing erection and took a step back, bumping into the door before she turned and fumbled for the doorknob.

"Cynthia."

"What?" she said, turning back to face me.

"The fruit...?" I reminded her.

"Oh! Shit. Yes. Thank you."

She moved around me back to the desk and picked up the tray.

"I'll...um...I'll text you later," she said, once she was back at the door.

"I'll be looking forward to it," I said.

She nodded, turned, opened the door and jumped when she nearly collided with Izzy, who was standing at the door, fist in the air as if she'd been about to knock.

"Oh! I'm sorry," Izzy said. She looked at me with a gleam in her eyes. "I was just coming to find you and see if you were ready to get back to it. I've got to take off soon. Stephen's about to get off work and Mom is watching Stephen Jr."

"Yeah," I said. "I'll be right there."

Cyn excused herself and took off, but Izzy continued to stand there, staring at me with a silly grin on her face.

I moved to the door and grabbed it. "Not one damn word, Isabella," I said before shutting the door in my nosy cousin's face.

"That is *gorgeous!*"

I jumped at the sound of Izzy's voice over my shoulder.

I'd been tucked away in a corner of the studio during the

shoot, lost in my sketch and hadn't even heard Izzy come up behind me.

I looked down at the sketch of the dress I'd been working on and then back up at Izzy.

"Oh...thanks. It's just something I like to mess around with in my free time," I said.

Izzy slid in the seat across from me. "Do you mind me taking a closer look at your designs?"

"Really?" I asked, surprised.

"Yeah! Unless you feel uncomfortable about it, then feel free to tell me to mind my own business."

"No!" I said eagerly, pushing my sketchbook over to Izzy.

I sat there, gnawing on my bottom lip, my hands clenched together on the table as I watched Izzy intensely study page after page of my work. Every once in a while, I'd notice one of her eyebrows raise and she'd give an approving nod or "hmm" before turning to another page.

Finally, she closed my sketchbook, looked up and passed it back to me.

"Cyn," she said, her voice full of admiration. "You are extremely talented."

"Wow...that...hearing that from *you*...wow."

"Have you ever brought any of these designs to life?"

I shook my head. "Drawing clothes is a piece of cake. But *making* them? Let's just say my execution has never quite been on point. I never got the hang of a sewing machine."

Izzy nodded her head in understanding. "Well," she said, tapping my sketchbook. "You have a gift."

"Thanks, Izzy," I said, pulling my sketchbook back towards me.

Izzy stood. "I'd better go check on Roman, Priscilla has been..."

"A handful?"

"I wouldn't say *that*," Izzy said, obviously trying to be nice.

"I'm sorry for any trouble she's been giving," I said.

"*You* have nothing to apologize for," Izzy said, cutting her eyes in the direction of Rome and Priscilla, the two of them seeming to be in yet another heated argument. She started to walk away and then stopped. "Hey, I know we don't really know each other so it's none of my business, but...your designs should be seen by the world. People should be *wearing* them."

And then she left me sitting there with a lot to think about.

Izzy certainly wasn't the first person to tell me that I should consider having my drawings turned into actual clothes.

Jaclyn, Octavia and Faye had all been trying to convince me to do it for years, but I'd always just waved it off.

Sketching had always just been a hobby of mine, something I did to get lost in and drown out everything around me that tried to drag me down.

I'd always loved to draw, but my fascination with clothes came when my father would let me tag along with him when he'd go to photo shoots or fashion shows with his clients. I'd have my sketchbook with me and I would draw my favorite outfits I saw the models wearing. Eventually, I started creating my own clothing sketches.

But instead of following my heart and majoring in art or design in college, I took what I assumed was the 'practical' route and majored in business, hoping it would help start me on my way to having some kind of successful career one day.

Yet here I was, years later, still at Priscilla's beck and call.

I let out a rueful sigh, as I looked up to see Izzy trying to play referee between Priscilla and Rome.

I watched as he ran a hand through his locs, a sign that he was irritated.

I thought back to our conversation in his office and how he'd made it abundantly clear that there'd never been anything between him and Priscilla. I felt like a fool for believing Priscilla and also felt like a complete jerk for the way I'd been acting towards Rome.

But he'd been quick to forgive, and I was grateful for that.

I smiled thinking about my charm that he'd found. It was safely tucked away in my purse and I had every intention on getting it properly fixed as soon as possible.

I pulled out my phone, went to my contacts and scrolled until I reached his name. He wanted to take me out for drinks later. I'd been hesitant, because of Priscilla, knowing she could summon me for something at any time.

But tonight...

I was gonna do like I'd done in Trinidad and live in the moment.

So I clicked on the message button and typed out a text to Rome.

I can meet you for that drink at nine tonight.

9

I walked into the bar that Rome had texted me the address to and looked around until I found him sitting in a booth in the back.

I weaved my way through the tables and when he looked up and saw me he stood to greet me.

"Hey," he said, smiling down at me.

"Hey," I replied back as I slid out of my jacket to reveal my dress.

"Wow, you look...amazing," Rome uttered as we slide into our seats in the booth.

"Thank you." The waitress came over and I ordered a lemon drop martini and Rome ordered a whiskey on the rocks.

"This place is nice," I said, looking around.

"Yeah. My brothers and I like to come here sometimes and hang out. My brother wants to get his beer sold here."

"Knight Brewery." I remembered seeing the building on my walk with Maggie the other day.

"Yep," Rome said, a hint of pride in his tone. "He got into craft brewing after he retired early from the NFL."

"And what about your other brother?" I asked, remembering that he was a triplet. "What does he do?"

"Ramsey's a muralist."

"Oh wow."

The waitress returned to our table with our drinks and I picked mine up and took a long sip.

"Sweet Rapids is such a beautiful town. Did you grow up here?"

"Sort of," Rome nodded. "After my father passed away, my aunt Irene convinced my mother to move here. She and my uncle Isaac helped raise us."

"That's good that you had someone who was willing to step in and take on that role in your lives."

We sat quietly for a moment nursing our drinks before I spoke again.

"Rome I can't thank you enough for finding my charm. I thought I'd never see it again."

"You don't have to keep thanking me, Cyn. I'm just glad I was able to do something to put a smile on that beautiful face of yours."

"I'll be smiling for days now thanks to this," I said, before I took another sip of my drink. When I placed my glass back down on the table, I looked up to find Rome staring at me.

"What?" I asked. I lifted my hand to my mouth. "Is there something on my face?"

Rome shook his head. "No. It's just...nice to see you like this."

"Nice to see me like what?"

"Like you were when we first met."

"Oh."

"I'm sorry," Rome said, placing his hands on the table in front of him. "I told myself I wasn't gonna ask. But I've gotta know."

"Know what?"

"How the hell can you work for someone like Priscilla Tremaine?"

My mouth dropped open at his question and Rome apologized again.

"I remember you telling me in Trinidad that you couldn't stand your job. And now *knowing* what your job is, I completely understand. But I just don't understand why you're still working for her."

My lips tipped up in a desolate smile. "It's a long, complicated story."

"I've got nothing but time."

I leaned forward, tracing the rim of my glass with my fingertip.

"Priscilla's my sister," I said quietly. I picked up the glass and finished off my drink.

"What?" Rome said, his eyes bulging wide.

The waitress came back and asked if we needed refills and we both nodded.

"Technically, stepsister," I continued after the waitress left again. "But my father adopted her so...yeah."

"Wait, wait, wait," Rome said. He shook his head and asked. "So...Frank Tremaine was your father?"

"Yeah," I said, my eyebrows slowly lifting.

"I knew Frank."

"What?" I asked in disbelief.

"I knew Frank," Rome repeated.

"Are you serious?"

"Yes!" Rome laughed. "When I was just getting started in

my career, he was one of the few people who gave me a chance. He gave me work, when I was still trying to build a portfolio." He blinked and pointed at me. "You're Bug!"

Hearing that nickname rocked me to my core.

It was my dad's nickname for me.

But it also brought a smile to my face.

"I can't believe that's how he referred to me to other people," I said, covering my face.

Rome smiled back at me. "He talked about you all the time. Bragged about how his bug, Cinnie, was away at college, making the Dean's List and was gonna do big things after she graduated."

That made me shake my head.

The waitress came with our second round of drinks and I scooped up my glass. "If he could see me now," I murmured before taking a long gulp of my drink. I placed the glass back on the table and let out a sigh.

"He'd still be proud of you," Rome insisted, reaching over to place his hand on top of mine.

"Thank you for saying that," I said quietly and Rome shrugged off my words.

"Just being honest," he said.

We stayed at the bar for another hour just hanging out and talking.

"I really enjoyed this," I said, as Rome walked me to my car.

"So did I," he said. "Maybe next time we could have dinner as well."

I opened my mouth already planning to use Priscilla as an excuse, but he cut me off with a kiss.

My hands instantly went to the back of his neck as his tongue slid into my mouth and his fingers sank into my hair.

"Just. Say. Okay," he quietly demanded, punctuating each words with an unhurried peck on my lips.

"Mmm...okay," I said, and he pulled away and looked down at me with a satisfied grin on his face.

"My place. Tomorrow night," he said, opening my door for me.

We actually had a few days off from the shoot, and Priscilla had already made plans to fly to Vegas with some of her friends. So it was perfect timing.

I slid into the driver's seat and Rome closed the door and gestured for me to roll the window down.

He leaned down into the window.

"Just so you know, by the end of the night, I plan on having a repeat of that night we shared in Trinidad together," he whispered into my ear, before planting a kiss on my lips that caused me to shiver.

"Shoot me a text when you make it in safely," he said, as he stood and took several steps back.

I nodded, rolled up my window and took off.

My mind was still reeling from Rome's words when I made it back to the house.

I'm here. I said in a text to him.

Can't wait until tomorrow night. -Rome

I grinned at his response and figured there was no point in beating around the bush.

Me neither.

Just remembering our time together in Trinidad...and the fact that fate was allowing us more time together made me giddy.

"Where the hell have you been?"

Priscilla's grating voice pulled me out of my moment of reverie and I'd had just enough to drink to not give a fuck.

"You know, Priscilla. When I'm off the clock, I really don't have to tell you a goddamn thing."

Priscilla's mouth fell open at my words.

"What the hell did you say—"

"And another thing," I said as I climbed up the stairs. "Don't forget, *I* am the older sister. Not you."

I left Priscilla standing there looking dumbfounded as I went to my room and slammed the door.

"So. What do you have planned now that the little brat has taken off for the next couple of days?"

I looked up at Faye and grinned.

Priscilla had taken off for Vegas earlier that morning, leaving Maggie and I in peace for the next two days. She had her bodyguard with her so I knew Priscilla wouldn't bother calling me while she was doing only God knew what. I decided to take advantage of my free time and called Faye to see if she wanted to meet for lunch and she immediately agreed. We made an entire afternoon of it with lunch and then a bit of shopping in Carson City at Izzy's clothing store. Now we were sitting in Everetts', the bakery I'd been eager to visit since my first stroll around the historic district of Downtown Sweet Rapids. I was excited to learn that they had a location in Carson City as well.

"This is gonna sound like something out of a movie or romance novel but...you remember the guy I told you I met in Trinidad?"

Faye immediately perked up.

"Yes!"

"Welp...seems it really is a small world, because he's the photographer over the photoshoot."

"Shut up!"

"I know. I'm having dinner with him tonight."

"It's a good thing we went shopping today then," Faye said with a wink and I laughed.

This time with my godmother was much needed and long overdue.

We were quiet as we finished off some of the best cupcakes I'd ever had.

"He knew Dad," I finally said, in a somber tone.

Faye looked up at me, surprise on her face.

"Really?"

I nodded, blinking away the sheen of tears that always arrived when talking about my father.

"He, umm, he apparently sent some clients Rome's way, when he was just starting out in photography. Helped him build his portfolio."

"That sounds like Frank," Faye said with a smile.

"Faye, I'm so tired of this shit," I blurted out. "Dad would have wanted more for me. *I* want more for me. This gig with Priscilla was only supposed to be temporary. It was never supposed to last this damn long."

"What are you gonna do about it then?" Faye asked.

"I think–" I amended that word when Faye rose a challenging eyebrow at me. "No. I *know* when we're done with this project, I'm quitting."

"It's about damn time," Faye said proudly. "This calls for more cupcakes."

"Did I hear someone say more cupcakes?"

We looked up to find Dana Everett, one of the owners of the bakery standing at our table.

"I was just coming by to see if you ladies were enjoying the cupcakes and if you needed anything else."

"Yes!" Faye said. "Let us get two of your margarita cupcakes."

"And can you box up four of your Better than Sex cupcakes?" I added.

"You've got it," Dana said before heading back to the front of the bakery.

"Do you have a plan for after you quit?"

"I've been thinking about putting my sketches together and building a fashion portfolio."

"Again, it's about damn time," Faye said, excitement lighting her eyes.

10

———

I checked the pot I had on the stove and let out a sigh of relief, thankful that everything seemed to be turning out right.

Once I got home from drinks with Cyn the night before, I realized that there was a small snag in my plan of having her over for dinner.

Cooking wasn't exactly my strong suit.

Luckily for me, I was related to one of the best chefs in the country.

I called Ian up and after he laughed his ass off at me and gave me grief, he gave me a recipe that he swore was foolproof.

"So far so good," I murmured to myself just as the doorbell rang.

I looked at the clock, my eyebrows furrowing when I saw the time.

Cyn wasn't due to arrive for another half an hour. I wiped my hands and headed for the door.

"Surprise!"

"Mom!" I said as I pulled the door open wider to let her in. "What, uh, what are you doing here?"

"Is that any way to greet your mother who you haven't seen in nearly a month?" she said, as she breezed past me and into my condo.

"Ma, you know I'm always happy to see you," I said. "It's just—"

"Something smells divine!" she gushed. She looked at me shocked. "Did *you* cook?"

"I threw a lil somethin' together," I said, rubbing the back of my neck. I looked at my watch again and followed my mother, who was making a beeline for the kitchen.

But she stopped when she got a look at my dining room table and noticed it set for two.

"Oh!" she said, pressing her hand to her chest. "You're having company."

"Yes."

She scanned me from head to toe and then excitedly said, "Female company."

She continued on to the kitchen.

"Mom, I don't mean to be rude, but you're kinda moving in the wrong direction."

"Hush up, this will only take me a minute."

Once she was there, she grabbed a spoon and removed the top off of the pot on the stove.

"We have to make sure you're not gonna poison the poor girl," she said, dipping the spoon into the pot. She gently blew on it before tasting it.

"Roman! This is absolutely divine."

"Thank you."

She put the spoon in the sink, and turned to look up at me, studying me again.

"You really like this girl, don't you?"

"Can we not do this right now?"

"Do what, boy?"

"The whole 'when are you gonna settle down like your cousins' speech."

My mother threw her fist on her hip and sucked her teeth at me.

"Now did you hear me say that, Roman Knight? No, all I asked was if you liked the girl. It's a simple question that requires a simple answer. Yes or no. And I already know the answer, 'cause you wouldn't be up here cooking one of your cousin's recipes if you didn't."

I was quiet for a moment before I nodded.

"Yeah, I do like her. A lot," I admitted, which made my mother's mouth tip up in a smile.

She reached up and straightened the collar of my shirt and fussed with my hair, which I groaned about and mildly swatted her hand away.

She let out a snicker of amusement and a little yelp when I pulled her into my arms for a tight hug.

"I missed you, woman," I said, kissing the top of her head.

"I missed you, baby," she replied patting me on my back.

"Now, you gotta go. She's gonna be here any minute, and I prefer her not to meet my mother on our sorta official first date."

"Okay, okay!" my mother said, as she moved out of our embrace and turned to head for the door. "Oh! I almost forgot."

She picked up the large gift bag that she'd put down when she first arrived and handed it to me.

I sat it on the foyer table and reached inside, pulling out

several shot glasses. It had become a bit of a tradition for my mother to bring me and my brothers shot glasses from each city she visited.

But I was surprised to see another gift in the bag.

"Mom..." I said, in awe. I looked up at her and she had a sweet smile on her face.

"I found it in the quaintest little store in Tuscany," she said, as I fondly examined the antique camera. "I thought it would be a nice addition to your collection."

"It's amazing," I said. I pulled her in for another hug. "Thanks, Mom."

"You're welcome," she said. "Now let me get out of your hair, before your little friend arrives."

I opened the door and walked her to her car. I watched as she drove off and gave her one last wave before I went back inside to finish dinner.

———

Not long after my mother left, my doorbell rang again.

This time it was exactly who I expected.

"Hi," Cyn said when I opened the door to greet her.

She looked incredible in a hip-hugging pair of jeans and a loose top that showed off one of her shoulders.

"Hey. Come on in."

She walked into the condo and I couldn't help but take the opportunity to admire the way her ass looked in those jeans as she walked past.

"Sorry I'm a little late, I had to make sure Maggie was set for the evening."

"Maggie?" I questioned, shutting the door behind me.

"Priscilla's dog. She left her with me while she took off to Vegas."

"Of course she did. Had I known I would have told you to bring her along."

"It's all good, my godmother is watching her for me."

"What ya got there?" I asked curiously, instantly recognizing the familiar box from Everetts'

"I didn't want to come empty-handed," she said, turning to face me. "So..." She held up the box and I smiled.

"While it was completely unnecessary, I'm never gonna turn down anything from Everetts'."

"Wow!" I followed her gaze and realized she was looking at the old camera on the foyer table. "That is a gorgeous camera."

"Thanks. It's a gift from my mother," I said, fondly running my fingers across it. I left out the fact that she'd just left not too long ago. "She got it while she was away on her latest trip. I collect old cameras."

"Where'd she go?"

"Tuscany."

Her eyes lit up. "Tuscany. Such a beautiful place."

"So you've been before?" I asked, moving closer to her.

"Yes. Unfortunately, I didn't get to truly appreciate it."

She didn't have to expand on her reasoning why.

I nodded in understanding. "You'll have to go again. For you."

"Maybe one day," she wistfully replied, as she took in a deep breath. "Whatever you're cooking, smells delicious."

"It's just about ready," I said, heading for the kitchen to check on everything.

"Do you need any help with anything?" Cyn asked.

"Nope, just make yourself at home. Would you like some wine?"

"I would love some," she said.

I grabbed the wine Ian advised me to pick up that would pair well with our food out of the wine fridge and two glasses.

After uncorking the bottle, I filled a glass and took it to Cyn. She took a long sip from the glass, and I went back to the kitchen to fix our plates.

"That looks so good," Cyn exclaimed as I brought the food to the dining room table and we sat down.

We fell into a companionable silence as we ate, and I was thankful that Cyn seemed to be thoroughly enjoying the meal.

"I can't get over how delicious that was," Cyn said, once we were finished. When we both stood at the same time, with our plates in our hands, I rose a questioning eyebrow.

"And just what do you think you're doing?" I asked.

"I'm helping clear the table," she replied, to which I was already shaking my head.

"Nah, gorgeous. You're a guest in my home, which means you don't lift a finger."

"But Rome, you cooked a fabulous meal. The least I can do is—"

"Go and chill on the couch," I said. "And grab those cupcakes. We can share dessert once I load the dishwasher."

She looked as if she wanted to argue, but then she smirked at me, and headed for the living room couch.

"Fine," she said, giving me a playful pout. "But next time, I'm helping and there's nothing you can do to stop me."

"I can think of a few ways," I teased, before turning to head for the kitchen, leaving her blushing.

As I loaded the dishwasher, I thought about how she'd said 'next time', as if she already saw us doing this thing again.

The thought of that brought a smile to my face.

I made quick work of cleaning up the kitchen, taking advantage of my open floor plan to sneak glances at Cyn here and there as she made herself comfortable in my space; kicking off her shoes and settling in on my sofa.

I started the dishwasher, wiped down the countertops, and went to join Cyn on the couch.

I grabbed the box from Everetts' off of the coffee table and opened it up. I reached in, grabbed a cupcake and handed it to Cyn and then took one for myself.

"Earlier you mentioned your godmother was watching Priscilla's dog?"

Cyn nodded. "Yeah, Faye lives in South Lake Tahoe. We actually spent the morning together, shopping, having lunch and checking out Everetts'."

"Sounds like a fun time."

"It was. I hate that I don't get to see her or spend more time with her, so this morning was great."

We both polished off our cupcakes and reached into the box for another.

"So," Cyn started as she peeled the wrapper off of the side of her cupcake. "Why photography?"

That question made me smile.

"Got my first camera when I was seven," I said. "It was a Christmas gift from my father. He and my mother realized I had a knack and a passion for it, so they continued to encourage me."

Cyn nodded and smiled back at me. "Having that support is...priceless."

"Yeah, it is," I said, staring at her as she finished off her cupcake. My gaze drifted to her wrist that held her charm bracelet. I reached out and grabbed her wrist. "You haven't put the charm back on yet?"

"Oh," she said, looking down at her wrist. "No, not yet. I haven't had a chance to get to a jeweler."

"Do you have your charm with you?" I asked.

"I do. It's in my purse."

"If you'd like, I can fix it for you right now."

"Seriously?" Cyn asked, her eyes lighting up.

"Sure," I said, standing.

Cyn hopped up, grabbed her purse and dug around in it

until she pulled out the charm. I unclasped the bracelet from her wrist and she handed me the charm.

"Oh yeah," I said after inspecting it and seeing that the ring was still attached to the charm. "This'll just take a minute. My tools are upstairs in my office."

We headed upstairs, and once we were in my office, I sat down at my desk, opened up a drawer and pulled out two pairs of flat-nosed pliers. I could feel Cyn hovering over my shoulder as I made quick work of reattaching the charm to the bracelet. Once I made sure it was tightly secured, I double-checked the rest of the charms to make sure there weren't any other loose ones. I tightened a couple, just to be on the safe side, and then stood and turned to face Cyn, who was eagerly staring at me.

I lifted her wrist and put the bracelet back on for her.

"There," I said, lifting her wrist to my lips. "All fixed."

"Thank you," she whispered, and I felt the slight tremble of her body as I softly kissed her skin.

I let go of her wrist and pushed a strand of her hair behind her ear. I eased my hand to the back of her neck and Cyn's eyes drifted closed as I kneaded the tightness away.

"You're tense," I murmured.

"Highly stressful job. But this..." she purred. "...feels amazing."

"Glad I can take some of your stress away."

Her head fell back and she let out a little moan that caused my dick to instantly spring to life. Unable to resist any longer, I pulled Cyn against my body and dropped my mouth down on hers.

My hands slid beneath her top as our kisses grew deeper and hotter.

"Cyn," I murmured against her mouth. "I want you."

I felt her head nod, and I lifted her into my arms and carried her to the bedroom. We wasted no time getting undressed, and once we were completely naked, I laid her down on the bed and climbed on top of her.

My mouth went to her neck licking, sucking and biting her in the spot that I remembered drove her crazy and made her wetter.

My fingers dipped between her thighs and I slid two fingers inside of her, drawing another moan from her.

I kept stroking her, rubbing the palm of my hand against her clit and I moved down to take one of her hard nipples into my mouth.

"Roman..." Cyn cried out, and something about hearing her say my whole name for the first time, caused my erection to grow even harder.

I continued kissing my way down her body, loving the way her stomach quivered as I ran my tongue along her delectable skin.

I pulled my fingers out of her and reached over to the night stand drawer to grab a condom and opened it.

"I haven't been able to stop thinking about you, since our time together in Trinidad," I said, as I slid the condom onto my dick.

"Me neither," Cyn admitted, as I spread her legs and eased my way inside of her, causing us both to let out a satisfied groan.

This felt...right.

Cyn felt right.

It was as if a part of me had gotten lost after we parted ways in Trinidad and now that she was here with me again...I'd found it.

I tried not to think too hard about what that meant; and instead I got lost in the moment. How good it felt to have her tight walls milking my dick with every single stroke.

My hands were gripping her thighs.

Her nails were scratching my back.

I felt her legs begin to quake and I knew she was on the verge of going over the edge.

She tried to tighten her legs around my waist, but I kept them wide open as I pummeled in and out of her over and over until she was screaming at the top of her lungs.

It only took a few more strokes for me to find my own release and then I rolled off of her and onto the bed.

Once my breath was back to normal, I cracked one eye open and looked over to find Cyn was already asleep, her light snores filling the room. I laid there watching her, her face looking serene and at peace.

I drew her body against mine, enjoying the way she felt in my arms and soon I was drifting off to sleep as well.

11

I was awakened by the smell of coffee filling my nostrils. I stretched my arms over my head, and then got out of bed. I ambled into the master bathroom to relieve myself and freshen up. When I was done, I went back into the bedroom, grabbing one of Rome's button down shirts and slipped it on before I went in search of him.

I inhaled deeply, a mixture of his cologne and his natural scent still lingering on the fabric of his shirt and memories of our night before filled my mind.

I'd been eager about being with Rome again from the moment he'd made his intentions clear. But I'd underestimated how much better it would be this time around.

I glanced over the stair railing that overlooked the entire

first floor and saw Rome moving around the kitchen. He looked sexy as hell, wearing nothing but a pair of pajama pants that hung low on his waist and his locs down around his shoulders. As if he sensed me watching him, he looked up at me and grinned.

"Good morning," he said.

"Good morning," I replied, making my way down the stairs and to the kitchen. "That coffee smells amazing."

Rome went and got another mug from one of the cabinets and handed it to me. He grabbed the coffee pot and filled my cup up for me.

"Thanks," I said.

"Do you need any cream or sugar?" he asked.

"Cream."

He nodded and went to the fridge.

"How'd you sleep?" he asked.

"Extremely well," I said, and he gave a sexy smirk, as he passed me the cream. I added a little, handed it back to him and he put it back in the fridge.

I took a sip and let out a content sigh.

"How long have you been awake?" I asked.

"Not too long," Rome said.

I turned and looked out the glass patio door, the early morning light casting a glow over the city and the mountains in the distance.

"I can't get over this view," I admired, as I took another sip of my coffee.

"Neither can I," I heard from behind me.

I smiled at Rome's words, knowing we definitely weren't talking about the same thing. I felt one of his arms loop around my waist and my head fell back against his shoulder as he pushed my hair to one side to gain access to my neck.

"You look really good in my shirt," he murmured, his fingers lazily dancing along my skin.

I shivered at the feel of his lips on my skin. "You don't mind me wearing it?"

"Not at all."

I turned in his arms and lifted my head, meeting his mouth for a coffee-flavored kiss, and he lifted me up onto the counter and stepped in between my legs.

"Do you have any plans for today?" Rome asked, gripping the countertop by my thighs.

"Nope," I said, planting my hands on his chest. "Priscilla probably won't head back to Sweet Rapids until late tonight."

"Good, 'cause I want you to spend the day with me."

"What do you have in mind?" I asked, my breathing becoming heavy as he pushed the shirt off my shoulders and kissed my collarbone.

"I want to show you around Sweet Rapids."

"I went on a little tour with Maggie when I first got here."

"You saw it through the eyes of a tourist," he informed me. "You haven't seen it through the eyes of a local."

"You...make...an extremely valid point," I breathed as Rome kissed his way further down my body, until his face was at the junction of my thighs.

Rome dropped to his knees and pulled me to the edge of the counter, pushing the shirt up around my waist. He pushed my knees apart and when I heard him inhale deeply, heated anticipation coursed through my veins. My legs trembled when he kissed my inner thighs.

At the first swipe of Rome's tongue along my clit, my back bowed and my hips jutted forward. That seemed to encourage him, because he began to drive me crazy with his mouth, sucking, slurping, dipping his tongue inside of me.

My hands went to the back of his head, gripping his hair as I rocked against his face, while he ate me out on his countertop as if I was the best fucking breakfast he'd ever had.

"Roman...I...I'm cum—" The words died on my lips as my

orgasm slammed through me, setting off frissons of pleasure over every cell in my body.

As I came back down, Rome began kissing his way back up my body, until he reached my mouth, giving me a wet kiss filled with my essence.

And then he lifted me off of the counter and carried me back upstairs to the bedroom.

The wind whipped through my hair and the late afternoon sun kissed my face as Rome and I rode through downtown Sweet Rapids on the bicycles he'd rented for us. After we spent the morning in bed, we swung by the rental house so I could change into some fresh clothes.

We had lunch at a diner named Lucy's and shared ice cream at a place called scoops.

When Rome first suggested we take the bikes, I'd given him some major side eye. Mostly because I, admittedly, hadn't ridden a bike since I was a kid; and even then, I hadn't been the best at it. But with his help it hadn't taken me much time to get the hang of it again and soon we were on our way.

We'd spent the better part of the afternoon exploring downtown with Rome showing me his favorite spots, all while snapping pictures of me every chance he got.

"Oh wow," I said, bringing my bike to a stop. I looked up at the large mural on the side of a building we were in front of. I shielded my eyes as I looked up to see a man up on scaffolding with a spray paint can in his hand.

"Looks like Ram is hard at work," I heard Rome say.

"Ram?" I asked.

"Yeah. Ramsey. My brother."

"Wait," I said looking over at him. "This is your brother's work? That's your brother?"

"Yeah. You wanna meet him?" Rome asked.

"Uhhh, yeah!"

"Hey asshat!" Rome shouted and I giggled.

"I don't think he heard you," I said, watching as he continued working, his head bobbing from side to side.

"He's probably got his ear pods in," Rome said, pulling out his phone and typing out a text.

A moment later, Ramsey stopped, pulled his phone out and then looked down at us and Rome waved at him. I watched as he climbed down and removed the mask from his face.

My eyes grew wide when I saw a carbon copy of Rome staring back at me. The only difference was their hair. While Rome's hair was in long locs down to his shoulders, Ramsey's was thick and tightly coiled on top of his head with a tapered fade.

"So this is who you kicked mom out of your place for yesterday," Ramsey said.

"What?" I gasped, turning to look at Rome in shock. "Roman, you didn't!"

"You talk too fuckin' much," Rome said to Ramsey. "Ram, this is Cynthia. Cyn, this is my brother, Ramsey."

"And the best looking triplet," Ramsey said, with a wolfish grin as he took my hand and planted a kiss on it.

"Careful," Rome warned Ramsey and Ramsey chuckled as he let go of my hand.

"Chill out, brotha. Damn." Ramsey stared at me for a second and then what appeared to be recognition lit his eyes. "Yo! Is this the girl from your ph–"

"We're gonna take off," Rome said, getting back on his bike, and I followed suit. "I'll see you later."

"Aight," Ramsey said with a knowing grin on his face. He then turned and looked at me. "Miss Cynthia, it was a pleasure to meet you."

"Likewise," I said. "And your mural is...amazing."

"Thanks. I'll holla at ya later, Rome," Ramsey said, before heading back to the scaffolding.

We soon took off and after a few minutes of silence, I asked, "He saw the pics of me?"

"Yeah," Rome answered. "Just the ones from Carnival, they were mixed in with all of the other pictures I took."

"Oh. That makes sense." People would want to see the photos that he'd taken during his vacation. I just happened to be in my fair share of those photos.

We rode a few more blocks and then Rome announced, "We're here."

We got off of our bikes, parked them in the rack designated for them and I read the sign on the storefront window.

"Aiden Hill Pottery & Gallery."

"Once a month they have a Sip -N- Sculpt night," Rome explained. "I managed to reserve spots for us, even though it's last minute. You game?"

"Hell yes!" I said, grabbing his hand and tugging him towards the door of the gallery. "I wanted to come and check this place out before, but I didn't want to go in with Maggie."

We went inside and I was in awe by all of the pottery and sculptors that were on display.

"Rome! You made it."

We turned to find a handsome man walking towards us and he slapped hands with Rome and pulled him in for a brotherly hug.

"Yeah, thanks for squeezing us in."

"It was no trouble; tonight's class isn't too full."

"Cyn, this is Aiden Hill, owner of the gallery. Aiden, I'd like you to meet Cynthia Tremaine."

"Hello, Miss Tremaine."

"Please, call me Cyn," I insisted.

"Cyn it is. Nice to meet you."

"Nice to meet you too."

"Let's head on back to the classroom and we'll get the two of you all set up."

We followed Aiden to a room full of high tables that were covered with clay and all kinds of tools.

"We're still waiting for a few more people," Aiden said. "But feel free to pour yourselves a drink and chill out for a few minutes."

We went over to the table that was set up with drinks and snacks and Rome poured us each a glass of wine, while I filled a plate up with appetizers.

"I haven't done anything like this since elementary school," I said to Rome.

"Me neither," Rome admitted as we returned to our table.

The last few participants trickled in and once everyone was settled, Aiden went and stood at the front of the class.

"Good evening," he said, grinning at all of us. He clapped his hands and rubbed them together as he asked, "Who's ready to create some art?"

"Your..."

"*Mug!*"

"Right. Your...mug. Looks—"

"Like shit," I chuckled, finishing Cyn's sentence.

"*No!*" she pressed. "It's...unique. Like Aiden said, 'there's no such thing as perfect, just create with passion'."

"Yeah, yeah. Tell me anything," I said as I wrapped an arm around her shoulders and pressed a kiss to her temple. "Meanwhile, your vase came out awesome."

"Thank you," Cyn preened as she held up the vase she'd created in class.

When Aiden first kicked class off, he told us that we'd be using air drying clay and informed us that there was no theme, and we were free to sculpt whatever we felt led to create.

I'd decided to make a mug, thinking it shouldn't be too hard. But the vision of what I wanted it to look like in my head versus what I'd actually made was different to say the least.

But I was still proud of my work, even though it wasn't the best looking thing.

"All that matters," I said. "Was whether or not you enjoyed yourself."

"And I did," Cyn said. "So much. Thanks for today."

"Thank *you* for hanging out with me today."

We reached the front door of Cyn's rental, and she looked up at me a hint of sadness in her eyes.

"I guess this is it," she said.

As much as I'd wanted to take her back to my place and spend another night making love to her, I knew it was wiser to bring her home, so we both could get some rest. It was back to work in the morning.

"Just for tonight," I said. "Cynthia?"

"Yeah?"

"I...like you. A lot."

I watched as she smiled up at me. "I like you a lot too, Roman."

"This thing between us...I want to continue exploring it. If you're down."

Cyn pulled her bottom lip between her teeth, and then nodded. "I'm completely down," she said and then she rose onto her tiptoes and lifted her head to kiss me.

I cupped the back of her head, tilting it so I could get better access to her mouth. Reluctantly, I slowly pulled away; knowing that if I kept it up I'd drag her into her place and do all of the things I really wanted to do to her.

"I'll see you in the morning," I said, pressing my forehead against hers.

"Okay," Cyn whispered, licking her lips. "Goodnight, Rome."

"Goodnight."

I watched as she pulled out her key, unlocked the door and went inside. I didn't head back to my car until I heard her lock the door.

As I drove off, I smiled to myself, thinking about how I'd taken a chance and just put it out there with Cyn, letting her know how I felt about us. I was glad to find out that she was just as interested in seeing where things went between us as I was.

There were definitely things we'd have to work around, like the fact that she lived in New York, and I was here in Nevada.

But it felt like the universe kept bringing us back together for a reason, and I was willing to do whatever it took to make this work if she was.

Far be it from me to fight with the universe.

12

I paced back and forth, checking my phone. I typed out a text to Rod, Priscilla's bodyguard, trying to figure out where the hell they were.

I'd been surprised when I'd gone to Priscilla's room to wake her, only to find her bed still made and no signs that Priscilla had yet returned from Vegas.

I called to see where she was and she belligerently told me she'd meet me at the studio.

Call time was three hours ago, and Priscilla still hadn't arrived at the studio.

Everyone was rightfully pissed.

Rome more than anyone.

I made my way over to where he was standing with Izzy, who was also visibly angry.

"Rome," I said, quietly. "I'm so sorry about–"

"Don't," he growled. "Don't apologize for her ass."

My mouth fell open, and Rome exhaled sharply and ran his fingers through his hair. He reached out and grabbed my wrist. "I'm sorry for my tone. But Cyn, this is ridiculous."

"I know. I *know*. I wish I could say this isn't like Priscilla."

"But we both know that would be a lie. We were just so close to being finished. I hoped we could get through this shoot without any bullshit."

"Me too."

"Why is everyone standing around?"

We all turned at the sound of Priscilla's voice. She came waltzing into the studio, shades on her face and I could tell simply by her complexion and her walk that she was completely hungover.

I marched over to her. "We're all standing around because you're three hours late, Priscilla."

"But I'm here now," Priscilla shot back. "So let's just...get this done."

Rome and Izzy walked over to us and I could tell that Rome was livid. But his tone was eerily calm when he said, "Priscilla, you need to leave."

Priscilla's eyebrows rose up above her shades. "Excuse me?" she spat out incredulously.

"You heard me," Rome said. "You come in here, three hours late, reeking of alcohol, rude as fuck and think that all that shit is gonna fly? Nah. Leave. Now."

"That's absurd. Yeah, I'm a little hungover, but it's nothing a little makeup can't fix," Priscilla argued.

"Let me say this so there is no confusion. Your services are no longer needed."

You could have heard a pin drop in the room as Rome and Priscilla stood toe to toe glaring at each other.

"You...you can't do that!" Priscilla shouted.

"Don't forget who's running this show. This is *my* shoot. At *my* studio. I can do whatever the fuck I want."

"I don't know if you're aware of this," Izzy piped in. "But the contract that you signed has a morals clause in it. And that clause states that if, at any time, you act in such a way that is deemed contemptuous, we have every right to terminate your contract."

"So," Rome said. "Consider your contract terminated."

Priscilla looked from Rome to Izzy, her mouth gaping open.

"B-but what about the photo spread? There's no way you're gonna find someone to replace me so quickly."

"You know just as well as I do that's not true. But I've already got someone in mind." Rome turned his gaze to me. "Cyn."

"*What*?!" both Priscilla and I exclaimed, though our tones were completely different. While Priscilla's was a screech of indignation, mine was pure shock and disbelief.

"You are not seriously going to make *her* my replacement," Priscilla said.

"What do you think?" Rome asked Izzy as if Priscilla wasn't even there.

Izzy studied me and nodded. "I'd have to take some of the outfits in a bit. But yeah, we could make it work."

That petty little jab set Priscilla off.

"This is ridiculous! Cynthia's no model. She's my fucking assistant," she spun on her heels and headed for the door. "If you're firing me, that means you're firing her. Where I go, she goes. Cyn, come. And you better believe you'll be hearing from my law—"

"No."

Priscilla froze and turned back to look at me.

"What. Did. You. Say?" she ground out through clenched teeth.

"First of all, don't talk to me like I'm a dog." I shook my head, rolling my eyes to the ceiling. "Ever since we were kids, all I've wanted to do was be an awesome big sister to you. One that you could come to for anything you needed. Somehow that morphed into me being nothing more than your doormat, catering to your every whim. And I am so *so* sick of this shit. I'm done."

"What?"

"You heard me. I'm done. Consider this my official resignation."

Priscilla snatched her shades off and stepped up to me, until we were nose to nose, rage in her eyes.

I felt Rome and Izzy surround me, Rome placing a protective hand on my lower back, and through its own volition, my body leaned closer to his.

Priscilla caught the subtle move and her eyes narrowed at Rome and me. She threw her head back and laughed. "*That's* what this is about! You're fucking her," she said to Rome. She looked back at me with a sneer on her face. "So you think you're suddenly special because he paid you a little attention? Guess what? You're not. You're just regular ass Cyn. You ain't shit, just like Frank wasn't sh—"

As soon as I heard my father's name fall from Priscilla's lips, I saw red. My fist connected to her jaw before I could even think to stop it. I heard Priscilla's yelp of pain, but I didn't give a fuck at this point. I dove at her and tackled her to the ground. I wanted to inflict as much pain on her as she'd inflicted on me over the years.

"Cyn! *Cynthia!*"

Rome's voice registered through the fog of anger I was

cloaked in and I felt his strong arms lock around my waist and drag me from off of Priscilla.

"You *bitch*!" she screamed at me, as Rod held her back. "You'll come crawling back. Just like you always do. You need us."

"I don't need a goddamn thing from you," I screamed back. "Not anymore."

"This is exactly why Mother kept Frank's will hidden from your ungrateful ass!"

I stopped fighting against Rome's hold and froze.

"What the fuck did you say?" I snarled.

Priscilla's eyes widened, realizing she'd obviously said something she shouldn't.

"Fuck this shit," she said, turning and heading to the door, Rod following behind her. "You'll be hearing from our lawyers."

"Priscilla, get your ass back here!" I yelled, but she kept walking. "What did you say about my father's will?"

I watched as Priscilla left and I stood there in shock.

Was what she'd said true?

"Cyn..."

I blinked and found Rome standing in front of me, concern in his eyes.

"We gotta get that hand iced, babe," Rome said.

I shook my head and backed away.

"I...I've gotta call Faye," I mumbled numbly.

"Okay," he said gently. "Let's go to my office. So you can have some privacy."

Needless to say, an entire crew had just seen me attack my stepsister. I was sure within the next few hours it would be all over the news.

But I couldn't worry about that now. I had more important things to worry about.

Like finding out if my father actually did have a will all this time and Linda had somehow managed to keep it hidden.

Faye was the only person who could help me.

Rome opened his office door for me and guided me in. "Take all the time you need," he said. "I'll be out front, but I'll come back and check on you later."

He quietly shut the door and I reached into my pocket to grab my phone. I winced as the pain in my knuckles began to set in.

But it paled in comparison to the pain I felt at the thought of Linda's betrayal.

This seemed diabolically low even for her. I'd always known that she disliked me and was envious of the way my father doted on me. But for her to go *this* far.

I wanted Priscilla's words to be false, some lie she'd thrown out in anger to hurt me.

But I already knew...

"Hey Cyn" Faye said cheerfully when she answered the phone.

"Faye," I whispered, my entire body trembling.

"What's wrong?" she immediately asked.

"Everything..."

"How are you?"

I stopped pacing and looked up to find Tessa Noble standing in the hallway. She ran Everetts' Bakery here in Sweet

Rapids and they'd been catering the breakfast baked goods and desserts for the shoot. She was also my cousin Isaiah's wife.

"How am *I*?" I asked, shaking my head. I looked at my closed office door. "I need to find out how *she* is."

"Why are you still just standing out here then?" Tessa asked with a soft smile.

I blew out a breath and ran my hand over the back of my neck.

An hour had gone by since the shit hit the fan between Cyn and Priscilla. After I'd brought Cyn to my office to call her godmother, I'd gone back out front and Izzy had been talking to the crew, sternly reminding them of the non-disclosure agreements they'd signed and that what had happened today was not to be talked about to any of the media.

I'd gone back to check on Cyn, but when I went to my office, I could hear her from outside, clearly upset as she talked to Faye on the phone.

"I just...I don't know." I shrugged. "Trying to give her some space, I guess."

"Maybe space isn't something she needs right now," Tessa suggested, as she moved closer to me. She pressed an ice pack into my hand and gave me a gentle nudge and an encouraging nod.

"Hey," I said, stopping to look at her before I went into my office. "I'm sorry your food went to waste today."

"It won't," Tessa said. "Some of the crew took some when Izzy sent them home. We'll take the rest to the shelter on the other side of town."

"Good," I said. I held up the ice pack. "And thanks."

"Let Cyn know we're here for her if she needs anything."

I nodded and then turned back to my office door. I gently tapped on the door, and slowly opened it, peeking my head inside.

I found her asleep on my couch, her face stained with dried

tears.

"Cyn," I said quietly after I went and sat down beside her. She let out a startled gasp and shot up swinging her arms. I grabbed her by the forearms to avoid her hitting me. "Whoa, slugger! I think you've knocked enough people on their ass for one day."

"Ugggh," she groaned and fell back against the couch. "I still can't believe I did that."

"You've got one hell of a right hook, Miss Tremaine," I said, taking her swollen hand in mine. She winced as I placed the ice pack on her hand. I went over to my desk and grabbed a bottle of pain killers out of the drawer and got a bottle of water from the mini fridge.

"Take these," I said, handing her the pills and opening the water for her.

"Thank you," she said.

"How are you holding up?" I finally asked, after she took the pills.

She shook her head, her eyes filling with tears. "I'm not, Roman. I'm not holding up at all. I feel like I'm falling apart."

I pulled her into my arms and wiped her tears away with my thumb. "That's okay, gorgeous. I've got you. I'm taking you back to my place and I'm gonna take care of you."

Cyn didn't argue, she just nodded her head against my chest.

"I'm going to let Izzy know and then we'll get out of here," I said standing, and leaving her on the couch. "Keep that ice on your hand."

I stepped out of the office and went to find Izzy.

"I'm taking her home," I said.

"Good," Izzy replied. "I would say to let her know she can stay in the rental house for as long as she needs, but I get the feeling she won't need it anymore."

The rental actually belonged to Izzy, who'd recently

purchased it and had it flipped and was now renting it out as a vacation home.

"No. She won't. But keep it on standby in case she decides she wants to go back."

Just because she was agreeing to go back to my place now, didn't mean she'd want to stay with me for however long she planned on staying in Sweet Rapids.

That was something I wasn't ready to think about either. She could damn well decide that she was ready to leave tonight and there was nothing I could really do to stop her.

"Iz, I'm sorry about everything," I said. "I know this might screw up your timeline for ever—"

"No, Rome," Izzy said. "If I would have just listened to you from jump...chosen someone else, this may have never happened. What's done is done now. All that matters now is making sure Cynthia is okay. Do you really think her step-mother did what Priscilla claimed?"

"They say the apple doesn't fall far from the tree," I said, growing angry for Cyn. "So knowing Priscilla, if her mother is anything like her then yeah. It wouldn't surprise me one bit."

"That's awful," Izzy sighed. "Go on, tend to Cyn. I'll swing by the rental and pick up her things and bring them over later."

"If Priscilla is still there—"

"I can handle Priscilla," Izzy assured me. "I'll see you soon."

"Okay," I said. "Lock up for me?"

"You got it. Oh! Her bag." Izzy went and grabbed it and gave it to me.

"Thanks," I said, taking the bag from her.

"No problem. See you tomorrow. Love you."

"Love you too."

I went back to my office and found Cyn still on the couch.

"You ready?" I asked.

"I need my bag," she quietly replied.

"Already got it," I said, holding it up for her to see. I went over to her and helped her up and walked her out to the back door to where my car was parked.

We were quiet on the ride back to Reno, and it didn't take long for Cyn to doze off in the passenger seat. When we got back to my place, I went around to the passenger side and scooped up a still sleeping Cyn, along with her bag, into my arms. I carried her into the house and up the stairs to my bedroom. I dropped her bag by the bedroom door and continued over to the bed, where I gently laid her down.

Her eyes opened, but they were still heavy with sleep.

"Rome?"

"Get some rest," I said. "I'll come back and check on you later."

She nodded and rolled over onto her side. I stared at her back for a moment and then moved to leave the room. I looked down and noticed that when I'd put Cyn's bag down when we first arrived some of her things had spilled out. I bent down, began putting everything back in the bag and my eyes landed on a sketchbook that had fallen out and open. I should have just closed it and put it away; it definitely wasn't my business. But instead I peeked over my shoulder to see if Cyn was still asleep. I could tell by the steady rise and fall of her back that she was, so I picked up the book. I had every intention of just looking at the page that the sketchbook was open on; but curiosity got the better of me and I found myself turning page after page, amazed by what I was seeing.

Cyn was an amazing artist.

I jumped when I heard Cyn let out a snore, and slammed the book shut.

I shook my head at myself and put her sketchbook back in the bag and put the bag on my dresser, before leaving the room, closing the door behind me.

13

My eyes slowly slid open and I was met with darkness. I sat up in the bed, Rome's bed and realized it was evening.

I'd slept most of the day away.

I rubbed my eyes, got out of bed and went to the bathroom. I turned on the light and was startled by my reflection. My hair was all over the place and my eyes were red.

I splashed some water on my face and ran my fingers through my hair before leaving the bathroom.

As I left the bedroom, I noticed my cellphone lighting up on the dresser next to my bag. I picked it up and saw the massive amount of texts, missed calls and voicemails from Faye, Jaclyn, Octavia...

And Linda.

I tossed my phone back onto the dresser, deciding to deal with it all later.

When I made it to the first floor, I noticed my suitcase from the rental house by the stairs.

"Izzy went by the house and got your things for you."

I looked over and saw Rome sitting on the couch.

"Please thank her for me the next time you talk to her," I said as I went to join him on the couch. "She didn't have to deal with..."

"No. Iz said she wasn't there," Rome said, closing his book as I sat down next to him. "Feeling any better?"

"Yes. No. I'm...all over the place."

Rome nodded as he sat his book down on the coffee table. "That's understandable, given everything that happened today." He reached over and took one of my hands between his. "How can I help?"

"I could really use a drink."

Rome's lips tilted up. He stood and headed for the kitchen. "How does tea sound?"

"Do you have any whiskey to add into it?"

"As a matter of fact, I do."

"Great. Forget the tea, just bring the whiskey."

Rome chuckled as he closed one cabinet and opened another. "Sure thing, gorgeous," he said.

He came back to the couch with two tumblers filled with ice. He sat the tumblers down on the coffee table and filled them both up and then handed one to me.

I closed my eyes as I took a long sip of the whiskey, letting out a sigh as the smooth spirit warmed my chest. When I opened my eyes again, Rome's concerned gaze was fixed on me.

"I spoke with my godmother," I started.

"Cyn, if you're not ready to talk–"

"It's fine," I assured him.

Rome nodded. "What did she say?"

"She said she'll handle everything. She's going to speak to a judge about getting a search warrant against Linda. Faye says if my dad left a last will and testament, Linda can either cough it up or face jail time."

"That's good," Rome said.

"Yeah," I said, swirling the ice around in my cup. "I just...I can't believe she would do something like this to me."

"People...suck sometimes."

"They really do," I agreed finishing off my drink.

Rome refilled my cup, and I let out a sigh.

"How's your fist?" Rome asked.

I held my hand up, opening it and closing it into a ball. "Better than earlier."

"The swelling has gone down," Rome said.

We sat on the couch in silence for a while.

Eventually, I spoke up.

"Can I ask you something?"

"You can ask me anything."

"Were you serious earlier at the studio? About me replacing Priscilla for the photo spread?"

"Completely."

"Rome. As much as I hate to agree with *anything* Priscilla says...she was right about one thing. I'm *not* a model."

Rome was quiet for a moment before he got up. I watched as he ran upstairs and a few moments later, he returned with his laptop.

"I want you to see this," he said, opening his computer. After he went through several clicks, he pulled up a folder with my name on it. I moved closer to him, as he scrolled through photo after photo of me.

"Cyn, I've said it to you several times already. The camera absolutely loves you."

"Maybe it's the man behind the camera."

He gave me a bashful smirk. "You make my job easy, gorgeous."

I couldn't deny that the photos *did* look amazing and I could easily see some of the pics he'd taken of me on our day date around Sweet Rapids as some kind of ad for something.

"I don't know, Rome."

"Look," Rome said, closing the laptop. "Given everything you've gone through today, I'll totally get it if you're not up for it. We can definitely find someone else to redo the shoot. But I know you can do this. And you'll do an amazing job."

I sat there thinking about it for a while.

"Well, I mean it's not like I have a pressing job I have to get to anymore," I said thoughtfully.

"Is that a yes?" Rome asked.

"Why the hell not?" I said. "Maybe it'll be just the distraction I need from...all this other bullshit going on right now."

"Are you sure?"

"Yeah," I said, nodding. "Yeah, I'm sure."

"I'll let Izzy know in the morning and we'll get the ball rolling." He put his laptop down on the coffee table and pulled me into his arms.

I sank into him, taking in his energy and we spent the rest of the evening like that, him holding me, talking to me, making me forget all the negative things in my life.

And it was pretty close to perfection.

The doorbell rang and I got up from the couch and went to answer the door. I fully expected it to be the delivery person with our pizza that I'd ordered, so I opened the door without even looking through the peephole.

"Bruh! I think I got it."

I jumped back to avoid getting trampled by Remi, who rushed into my apartment with a six pack of bottled beer.

"Remi," I said, shutting the door and following behind him. I looked up to the second story. "Now's *really* not a good time."

Cyn and I had spent the day together lounging around at my place. After I'd called and let Izzy know that Cyn was down to do the shoot, Izzy had sent over a gift basket for Cyn filled with all kinds of products from Noble Naturals.

Cyn had taken advantage and decided to take a long soak in my oversized tub.

Remi followed my gaze and swore.

"Shit. Is your lady here?"

"She's not my...Yeah. She is."

It was the first time Cyn had been referred to as 'my lady'; and while I was initially going to correct Remi and tell him that she wasn't, it sounded too damn good to deny.

"My bad," Remi said. "I should have called before swinging through."

"Yeah, you should have. We've been...kickin' it around the house today. Keeping it low key after yesterday."

"What happened yesterday?" Remi asked.

"You hadn't heard?" I was honestly surprised. I figured word would have gotten around the family grapevine by now.

I gave my brother a brief rundown of what had happened between Cyn and Priscilla.

"Fuck," he said when I was finished. "That's...a lot of shit to deal with."

"Yeah it is," I said. "So if you don't mind..."

"Yeah, yeah. I got you, bruh. But Imma leave the beer and you guys give it a try and call me later to let me know what you th—"

"Rome? Is the pizza here?"

Remi and I both turned to find Cyn coming down the stairs. She stopped, blinked and smiled.

"You must be Remington," she said.

"How'd you know?" Remi asked, grinning at her.

"The hair," Cyn said, and Remi ran his hand against the smooth low-cut waves.

"That's right! Ram told me that he met you the other day."

"And it's nice to finally meet you as well," Cyn replied, stopping in front of Remi and holding her hand out. Remi took her hand and shook it.

"Same," he said. "And please, call me Remi."

The doorbell rang, and this time it actually was the pizza guy. I went to answer the door as Remi let go of Cyn's hand.

"I'm gonna take off," he said. "I just came by to drop off some of my latest batch of ale for Rome to taste test."

"We just ordered some pizza, if you want to stay," Cyn offered.

"Oh, I don't wanna intrude," Remi said.

"Then don't," I grumbled, slamming the door shut.

"Roman," Cyn chastised me before turning back to Remi. "You would not be intruding."

I sat the pizza down and pulled Cyn off to the side.

"You do *not* have to entertain his lame ass."

"You know I can hear you," Remi said, already opening the pizza box and grabbing a slice for himself.

"Really nigga," I said, looking at him as if he was crazy.

"What?" Remi asked with a mouth full of pizza.

Rolling my eyes, I shook my head and turned back to Cyn, whose eyes were lit with amusement. *That* was something I was glad to see.

"Rome," she said, lifting her hand to palm my face. "It's fine."

I took a deep breath in and could smell whatever products she'd used from Izzy's gift basket on her body and hair. She smelled like Remi needed to get the fuck outta my house so I could take her upstairs and taste her again.

As if reading my mind, Cyn grinned, and whispered, "There's plenty of time for that later." She pressed a kiss to my cheek and moved around me to join Remi. "Do you mind if I try your beer too?"

"Not at all," Remi said. He picked up one of the bottles from the carton, popped the bottle cap off and handed it to her. "Because you had more manners than my heathen ass brother, you get the first one."

"Thank you!" Cyn said, before bringing the bottle to her lips. "Oh. Remi, this is *good*."

I grabbed a bottle, opened it and took a long swig. I nodded my head.

"This shit is amazing Remi."

"Yes!" Remi said, clapping his hands. "This is it. This is the signature beer for Knight Brewery."

"I think you're right," I said. "Congrats, bro."

"I gotta get some bottled for Ian to try soon," Remi said, more to himself than us. "I heard he'll be wrapping up the cooking competition show in L.A. soon and will be back home in a few weeks."

We all sat down at the table and dove into the pizza and spent the rest of the evening hanging out.

It felt good to see how well Cyn got along with my brothers.

After a few hours, Remi made his exit.

"Thanks for letting me crash your evening," he said to Cyn, pulling her in for a hug.

"Thanks for the beer," Cyn said. "I can't wait to try your other flavors."

"You'll have to come to the grand opening next month. If you're still in town by then."

"Oh," Cyn said. "I...um...I guess we'll see."

Remi nodded, and turned to me. We clasped hands and leaned in for a hug before he turned and headed down the walkway to his car.

I shut the door and turned to find Cyn with a solemn look on her face.

"Now what's got you looking like that?" I asked, caressing her cheek with my knuckles. "Was it something Remi said? Cause I'll go out and put my foot up his ass."

"No!" Cyn laughed. Then she let out a sigh. "It's just...With everything going on, I guess I didn't think about the fact that I'll have to go back home to New York at some point. Which means that you and I will–"

"Make it work," I said, cutting her words off. "It just means we'll make it work."

Cyn looked up at me, and my words seemed to soothe her.

"We'll make it work," she agreed with a nod.

"Now," I said, lifting her up into my arms, causing her to let out a yelp. "We've got some unfinished business upstairs."

14

"Ugh. I still can't believe Linda's awful ass did that to you," Octavia fussed.

I was on a group video chat with Jaclyn and Octavia, filling them in on everything that had happened.

"*I* can't believe you beat Priscilla's ass," Jaclyn cackled. "What I would have paid to see *that*."

I shook my head and bit my lip to hide my amused grin.

It was just what I needed after the text I'd received this morning from Faye. Four simple words that, although were kind of expected, gutted me.

We found the will.

Faye had also let me know that she'd filed a lawsuit on my behalf against Linda for knowingly withholding my father's will and would let me know when a court date was set.

"You know if we could, we'd be out there with you," Octavia said, giving me a soothing smile.

"Shit. Her ass don't need us," Jaclyn teased. "Not with her being all shacked up with her photo bae."

"I'm not...shacked up," I denied.

But the truth was...it had been several days and I was still at Rome's place. So maybe I *was* sorta shackin' up with him. But he didn't seem to mind. Not once had either of us mentioned me going back to the rental house since he'd brought me to his place after the incident with Priscilla.

"Mmhmm, whatever," Jaclyn said. "Long as he keeps that glow on ya face, we're happy for you, sis."

"You really do look a lot less stressed," Octavia pointed out.

"Good dick and no longer working for an awful bitch will do that," Jaclyn said.

"You know I really, *really* can't stand your ass," I giggled.

"And we know that's really, *really* a lie. But whatever you need to help you sleep at night," Jaclyn teased.

"I'm sure photo bae is helping her sleep just fine," Octavia chimed in and she and Jaclyn fell into a fit of laughter.

"Whatever, I'm about to go," I said. "I love you guys."

"We love you too," they both shouted.

"Send us the pics from the shoot!" Jaclyn added.

"I'll see what I can do," I promised before hanging up.

It felt good talking to my girls. They always had a way of making me feel so much better.

I sat there for several minutes alone in Rome's room gazing out the window, taking in the beautiful mountain back drop.

Despite everything that had gone on in my life in the last few days, I realized that I'd still managed to find something I hadn't had in a long time.

Peace.

And while Rome had been a large reason for that peace, it was hard to deny the fact that the location played a profound role in that as well.

I was going to miss Rome whenever I did finally leave, but I was slowly beginning to realize that I was going to miss Nevada too.

———

"You can still change your mind."

I looked up at Rome as we walked hand-in-hand down the sidewalk.

"You were the one advocating for me to do this," I reminded him.

"And I still want you to. Only if you're absolutely sure. The last few days have been...a lot for you," he said.

His concern for me was endearing. He'd been so attentive over the last few days, making sure I was well taken care of.

"Yes," I agreed. "They have been a lot. But thanks to you, I've had way more good moments than bad."

"I'm happy to oblige, gorgeous," Rome said, pulling me against his body and lowering his mouth to mine for a sweet kiss. "Okay, let's get started."

He pulled the door open to his studio and we were immediately surrounded by a swarm of people. Izzy led the charge of makeup artists, hairstylists and her assisting designer/seamstress. She looped her arm through mine and tugged me away from Rome.

"She's in good hands," Izzy called over her shoulder as we moved in the opposite direction from Rome. She looked at me excitement lighting her eyes. "I hope you don't mind but Rome showed me some pics he took of you the other day. I noticed you wearing a dress from my latest line and *girl!* You looked fierce! I can't wait to see you in all of the outfits I have planned for you."

The next few hours were a blur as I had several people working on me at the same time. I'd been on the spectator side of this scenario more times than I could count with Priscilla. But to be able to sit and be pampered from head to toe before being dressed by one of my favorite designers herself was indescribable.

Izzy took a step back and looked up at me from the pedal stool I'd been standing on and gave me a nod.

"You ready?" she asked.

I turned and looked at myself in the full mirror. The first outfit Izzy had put me in was a simple tank top and jeans.

"As ready as I'll ever be," I said, nerves finally starting to kick in. It was finally starting to sink in that these photos would be seen all over the world as advertisement for Izzy's brand.

"You'll be fine," Izzy said. "Roman will make sure of it."

I nodded and took Izzy's hand to help me down off of the stool.

"Rome!" she called out. "We're ready."

Rome walked over to us, fidgeting with his camera. When he looked up he stopped in his tracks and just stared at me.

His heated gaze roamed my body from head to toe, and I tried not to fidget from his scrutiny.

Finally, he cleared his throat and smiled at me. "Let's get started."

He led me over to the set and had me stand in front of the backdrop. He pulled his phone out, pushed a button and the studio filled with music. He reached out and adjusted the strap of my top.

"Cyn."

"Huh?" I said, blinking at him.

"Breathe, babe," he said.

I let out a long breath and he gave his first instructions on how he wanted me to pose. He made it easy and fun, shouting out cues, telling jokes, anything to make me feel more comfortable.

I changed outfits several more times, the final outfit being a midi length body con dress.

"Look over your shoulder at me, Cyn," Rome ordered. I did as I was told and he snapped a few pics. "Yes! Perfect. That's a wrap for today. Tomorrow we'll do the outdoor shoot."

Izzy was coming out with an athletic line of clothes, and that had been what the outdoor photos had been centered around. From what Rome told me, Priscilla's pictures hadn't come out that great and he and Izzy had already been discussing doing a reshoot of that set of photos before they'd let her go.

They'd both seemed to be way more confident in my ability to do a better job than Priscilla than I'd had in myself.

But after today's shoot, I was a lot more at ease than I'd been beforehand.

Izzy rushed over to me and wrapped me up in a hug.

"Oh my goodness, you did so goooood!" she raved.

"Yeah, she did."

I turned to find Rome staring at me, that same look he'd had before the shoot started.

"Miss Tremaine, may I speak with you in my office, please?"

"Umm, yes. Of course," I stammered. I pulled out of Izzy's embrace and turned towards Rome. He rested his hand on my lower back and guided me to his office.

We went inside and I turned to face him as he closed the door.

"Is something wr—" I couldn't finish my question before he closed the distance between us and took my face between his hands as his lips came crashing down on mine.

I threw my arms around his neck and wrapped my legs around his waist when he lifted me into his arms and carried me across his office.

He planted me on top of his desk and shoved the dress I was wearing even further up until it was bunched up around my waist. I tugged his belt open, and after I unbuttoned and unzipped his pants, I slid my hand inside of his boxers and wrapped my hand around his throbbing erection.

"Goddamn, woman," he hissed as I stroked him over and over, running my thumb over the tip of his dick.

Eventually he pulled away, shoved his pants down and then grabbed my thighs, yanking me closer to him. He shoved my thong to the side and slammed into me, causing me to let out a scream. I gripped the edge of Rome's desk as he moved in and out of me at a frenzied pace. I could hear items falling off of his desk, but he didn't seem to be fazed by it, so I let my head fall back, and enjoyed the feel of his lips on my neck, his teeth digging into my skin followed by his tongue lapping at the same spot to soothe the sting.

Rome suddenly pulled out completely and stood me back up. When he spun me around and bent me over his desk, my pulse skyrocketed. He entered me again, gripping my hips as he went back to pounding into me over and over again.

I met every one of his thrusts with my own, my ass slapping against his stomach. My back arched when I felt Rome's hand in my hair, tugging just hard enough to send a multitude of tingles rocketing through my body.

"Roman..." I breathed, feeling my body begin to vibrate. Rome slid a hand between my thighs and when his fingers circled my clit, I exploded.

After several more pumps, Rome pulled out and came on my back.

"Don't move, gorgeous," he said. I heard him pull his pants

up and then a few moments later, I felt him wipe me down with a warm towel.

"You're good," Rome informed me and I stood and pulled my dress back down. He reached out and pulled me into his arms. "You were looking so damn amazing today. I just had to have you."

I shivered as he kissed my neck.

"And have me you did."

"But seriously," Rome said, looking down at me. "You killed it out there today."

"Thank you," I replied.

"Come on," he said, taking my hand in his. "Let's get out of here and go get some dinner."

15

"Cyn, can you rest your elbow on that rock? Yeah. Now lean back just a little bit. Perfect."

I snapped several pictures of Cyn in the sports bra and matching shorts from Izzy's new workout apparel line, Sweatin'.

Cyn had been doing amazing all day. Whatever cue I threw out to her, she was down to do. I'd gotten a lot of great photos of her, including some shots of her jogging, that still had me low key panting over her sexy ass.

But the way she was sitting on the ground, gazing out over the mountain's edge that overlooked a lake, while the sun made her skin glisten...

She was fucking radiant.

The fact that I wouldn't get to see her or touch her every damn day soon had me in my feelings.

Cyn's godmother had sent a text this morning, letting her know that the court date was in a few days, which meant Cyn had to head back to New York the day after tomorrow.

We had one more day of shooting – a few pieces from Izzy's bridal collection – and then we'd be done. I was hoping to get that finished early in the day, so I could have Cyn to myself before I had to take her to the airport.

"That's it for today," I called out after I got a few more shots. "Call time is six a.m."

I went and held my hand out to help Cyn up.

"Six a.m. Really?" she groaned.

I chuckled as we took our time walking down the mountain to my SUV.

"Well," I reminded her. "We're getting a mix of photos of you both in the studio and at several locations around Sweet Rapids."

"I know," she sighed. "This modeling shit is just...intense."

"Yeah, but you've done an outstanding job. Got me thinking about using you for other projects."

Cyn was already shaking her head. "Oh, no! Consider this a one and done favor, sir. This was fun, don't get me wrong. But I prefer being behind the scenes much more."

"You mean like designing clothes?" I absently asked.

Cyn stopped walking and stared at me.

"You saw my sketchbook?"

I stopped and turned to face her.

"I...yeah," I admitted, shoving my hands in my pockets. "I'm sorry, I wasn't trying to pry. When I brought you home the other day, a bunch of stuff fell out of your bag, including your book. When I went to pick it up, I noticed your sketches."

"Oh." She looked away from me. "What...uhh...what did you think of them?"

"They were amazing."

Her gaze met mine again.

"You really think so?" she asked.

"I wouldn't lie to you."

She stared at me for several long moments, rubbing her upper arms. Finally, she said, "Thank you, Rome. I have been thinking of putting together a portfolio of my sketches and checking out some fashion houses to apply for jobs for."

"Cyn, that's great."

I wanted to tell her that there was a great fashion house right here in Sweet Rapids and I was pretty damn close to the owner; but I got the feeling she'd know it was my low key way of trying to find a way to get her to stay here, and I wasn't sure how she'd react to that, so I kept my mouth shut. Our relationship was still so new, I didn't want to risk freaking her out.

We started walking again and after a few minutes of silence, I said, "If you don't mind, I'd like to see some more of your designs."

I could hear the smile in her voice when Cyn said, "Sure. I'd love to show them to you."

The light tapping on my door, snapped me out of my focus on the photo I'd been editing. I looked at the clock on my computer and noticed that it had been two hours since we'd arrived at the studio.

Like they'd done every other day of the shoot, Izzy and her style team had taken Cyn to get ready.

"Mr. Knight," Izzy's assistant, Trina, spoke up. "She's ready for you."

"Thanks, Trina," I said, grabbing my camera.

"She looks sooo beautiful," Trina sighed as I stood and

headed for the front of the studio. "I will *definitely* be buying from the Izzy's Bridal Collection."

"That's what's up," I mumbled as I went through my usual photoshoot camera pre-check. "Alright folks, last day of the shoot! Let's make it the be—"

My heart slammed in my chest when I glanced up and saw Cyn.

Even with Trina going on and on about how beautiful Cyn looked in the wedding dress, I still hadn't been prepared.

She was breathtakingly stunning.

I took my time making my way over to her, taking in every inch of her. She hadn't noticed me yet, since people were surrounding her doing their final touch ups. But they quickly moved out of the way once I arrived and stopped right in front of Cyn.

"You...look..." I shook my head.

Cyn smiled and shyly looked away, her cheeks flushed. I lifted my camera and quickly snapped a couple of pictures of her.

I moved in closer and moved a few strands of her hair and adjusted the veil she was wearing, letting my fingers graze her fully exposed shoulders.

"Isn't it bad luck to see the bride in her dress before the wedding?" Cyn teased. Then her eyes widened and she nervously shook her head. "That was a terrible joke. Way too soon for anything like that. I don't know why I—"

I stopped her stammering by leaning in and pressing a kiss to her lips.

"You're good, gorgeous," I said, grinning at her.

"Fuck! Really Rome?! Can someone please fix Miss Tremaine's lipstick?" Izzy yelled. As she walked off, I heard her grumble, "It's bad enough they had to put a pound of makeup on her neck."

She was obviously referring to the passion marks I'd left on Cyn's neck.

"You're in troooublllleee," Cyn whispered.

"Totally worth it," I said, winking at her as I backed away to let a makeup artist reapply some more lipstick to Cyn's lips.

A few minutes later, she was ready again and I started shooting.

Cyn was a natural, once again making my job easy. She changed dresses several times, and she looked amazing in every single one. We finished shooting indoors and headed out to get several shots around Downtown Sweet Rapids. I got shots of her strolling down the sidewalk with a bouquet of flowers, standing in front of store windows and I even got a great pic of her in the middle of the street.

My favorite photos were of Cyn standing in front of a water fountain in one of the city's parks.

"And that is a wrap!" I shouted and the entire crew began clapping. I went over to Cyn took her hand and lifted it in the air, and the applause grew louder.

"You did a spectacular job this week," I told her.

"Thank you," Cyn said quietly.

"You ready to get out of here?"

"Yes!"

"Let's go."

"*Fuuuck,*" Rome groaned, his hands digging into my hair as I took his dick even further down my throat.

After we'd finished the shoot, we'd gone back to the studio, so I could change back into my clothes. I'd been taken by surprise to find out that Izzy had put together a small party for me as her way of thanks.

I appreciated the gesture, and I enjoyed myself at the party, but I was more than ready to go back to Rome's place. Especially since we didn't have much time left to be alone. So when he came over to me after about an hour and whispered into my ear asking if I was ready to go, I gave him an emphatic yes, hugged Izzy and told her goodbye with a promise to keep in touch.

We couldn't get back to his place fast enough and the door to his apartment had barely closed before we started tearing each other's clothes off.

I looked up at Rome and found his hooded gaze on me while I continued sucking him. I tightened my grip around the base of his dick and pulled out, licking the tip before taking him in my mouth again, causing his hips to thrust forward as he let out a growl.

He pulled out, flipped me onto my back and eased inside of me. I let out a moan, loving the feeling of no barrier between us.

After we'd had sex in his office the other day, we discussed how we'd gone without a condom. We assured each other that we'd both been tested and were clean and I also told him I was on the pill. We hadn't used one since then.

My fingers fisted the sheets as Rome slid in and out of me with slow, unhurried strokes. His hands were everywhere: in my hair, on my breasts, around my neck. He leaned down and captured my lips in a mind-numbing kiss as our hips rolled back and forth against one another.

He gripped my ass and tilted my hips, driving even deeper

into me and my head fell back against the pillow, my body writhing beneath his.

"Roman," I moaned, opening my legs even wider, as heat coiled in my belly.

His pace gradually sped up and I knew he was close. Rome buried his head into my neck and I wrapped my arms around his wide back, holding on for dear life as we came together.

Our labored breathing eventually returned to normal and Rome finally rolled from on top of me and pulled me into his arms.

"What are you thinking?"

I opened my eyes and looked up at Rome.

"I was just thinking 'haven't we been here before'," I said quietly.

I heard him sighed and he tightened his arms around me. He knew exactly what I meant. I was heading back to New York in the morning.

"Yeah, I guess we kind of have been here before. But things are different this time," Rome said. "This time when we say goodbye...it won't be for good."

We'd already exchanged all of our contact information to keep in touch.

I nodded my head, feeling comforted by his words, and I snuggled deeper into his hold as he stroked my back until I fell asleep.

Sadly, morning came much too soon.

After getting up, showering and sharing what could only be described as an extremely solemn breakfast, Rome drove me to the airport to catch my flight.

I morosely watched Rome get out of the SUV and come around to my side to open the door for me. I placed my hand in his outstretched one and got out of the vehicle. I stood on the sidewalk while Rome went to the back and got my suitcase.

He sat it down next to me and I tried to look away, my eyes misting over.

"Cyn. Cynthia, look at me," he coaxed. He gently lifted my chin up, forcing me to look at him. He brushed away a stray tear with his thumb and gave me a soft smile. "Uh uh. No crying, gorgeous."

His hand moved to my neck and he brought his lips down to mine.

I wrapped my arms around his neck and held on, until he eventually broke the kiss and took a step back.

"Call me when you land," he said, and I nodded.

I grabbed the handle of my suitcase, turned and made my way into the airport.

I made it through security with, thankfully, no hassles and found my departure gate.

Once I found a seat, I put in my earbuds and turned on my music. I pulled out my sketchbook and got to work on a new design. Being around Izzy had been inspiring and I was looking forward to the new possibilities that were lying in wait for me.

Including the possibilities with Roman Knight.

16

"Y ou ready for court tomorrow?"

I sighed at Rome's question. We'd talked or video chatted every day since I'd left Sweet Rapids and even though it felt good to still be connected to him, it just wasn't the same as being *with* him.

I missed him...a lot.

"I'm just ready for this to be over," I said.

"I get it. And it will be soon, gorgeous. Hey good news, I finished editing your photos."

"You did! I can't wait to see them."

My doorbell rang and I looked up confused. I wasn't expecting company this evening.

"Rome, hold on," I said, getting up from the couch and

129

going to see who was at my door. When I looked through the peephole and saw who it was, I gasped, dropped my phone and yanked the door open.

"Hey, gorgeous," Rome said, grinning at me, looking as sexy as ever.

I excitedly leapt into his arms, wrapping my arms around his neck and my legs around his waist and planted a huge kiss on his lips.

"What are you doing here?" I asked, as he walked inside and kicked the door closed.

"Had some meetings," Rome said. "Figured I'd come surprise my girl and also be here for moral support if she needed me."

It felt good to hear him refer to me as 'his girl'.

"I so *so* needed you," I said, as I continued kissing him. "I've missed you."

"I've missed you too," he said, as he carried me over to the couch. He laid me down and slid his hand under my shirt, palming my bare breast. He shoved my shirt up and replaced his hand with his mouth, sucking, licking and biting my nipple until it hardened.

He slipped his hand into my sleep shorts and slid his fingers between my slick folds, strumming me, making me wetter and wetter.

He sat up to undo his pants, pushed them down and I lifted my hips so he could pull my shorts off. He gripped his dick and I watched him stroke it several times before he rammed into me, the mixture of pain and pleasure setting my body on fire. He tossed one of my legs over his shoulder and pressed a kiss to my ankle as his hips ground against mine over and over again.

"Rooomaaaan," I cried out as he plunged deeper inside of me. He leaned down and grabbed my face for a kiss, capturing my tongue with his.

My entire body sizzled as he drove into me harder and faster until I reached my peak. My pussy clenched around his dick and after a few more pumps he collapsed on top of me.

I kept my body tangled around his, loving the feel of his weight on top of me, his cologne intoxicating me; but eventually he got up.

I opened my eyes when I felt him lift me into his arms.

"Where's your bedroom?" he asked, and I pointed him in the right direction.

"I still can't believe you're here," I sleepily murmured.

"I'm here, gorgeous," I heard him say before he pressed a kiss to my forehead. "I'm here."

"She can have the company."

My eyes widened at Cyn's words to the judge.

Faye, whom I'd met before we'd gone into the courtroom, looked just as shocked.

"Umm, your honor? May I have a brief word with my client?"

"I'll allow it," the judge said.

I watched as Faye and Cyn whispered back and forth intensely. My gaze drifted to the other side of the court where Cyn's stepmother, Linda, along with Priscilla – who was still rocking one hell of a shiner on her left eye – sat with a smug smirk on her face.

When we'd first arrived at the courthouse earlier that morning, Linda and Priscilla had gotten there at the same time. Cyn and Linda facing each other had been strained, and neither of them had spoken to each other. But it hadn't been lost on me the way Priscilla had glared at me and then leaned over and whispered something to Linda, which caused Linda to look me up and down with antipathy-filled eyes.

I looked back over to Faye as she sighed and spoke up.

"Your honor, as my client stated earlier, she is willing to let Mrs. Tremaine continue running Tremaine Modeling Agency," Faye reluctantly said.

The judge looked at Cyn.

"Miss Tremaine...are you *absolutely sure* this is what you want to do?"

Cyn cleared her throat and stood.

"Yes, your honor. I loved my father and he meant so much to me. But this company was never my passion. And while my stepmother and I don't necessarily see eye to eye on much of anything, I can't deny that she is more than capable to run this business, much better than I ever could. So I'll give up my controlling interest in the company, by selling her my shares. However, I would still like everything else that was promised to me in the will."

"That is *more* than fair," the judge said. She turned her gaze to Linda. "Mrs. Tremaine. In light of everything presented to me, I have to say I am absolutely appalled. The fact that you *purposely* kept your husband's will hidden all these years, just to keep your stepdaughter from receiving her inheritance is utterly disgraceful. While Miss Tremaine has been *exceptionally* generous towards you in this situation, I still feel like you need to face some consequences to your actions. With that being said, the court finds you in contempt and orders you to serve five hundred hours of community service."

"This is ridiculous," Linda mumbled.

The judge's eyebrow arched up in surprise.

"Oh, I'm sorry," she said. "Since there is obviously something wrong with my ruling, let me try again. Thirty days in jail."

"*What?!*" Linda screeched as she shot out of her seat.

"How about we make it sixty days in jail?" the judge challenged.

Linda's temper flared and her eyes landed on Cyn. "You would have run the company into the ground! *I'm* the one who brought that company back to life, because your father was too damn focused on your pitiful ass to properly run it."

"Ninety days. And an additional five hundred hours of community service," the judge roared. "Bailiff, get Mrs. Tremaine out of my courtroom."

"*Mother!*" Priscilla screamed as the bailiff walked towards Linda. She looked at the judge. "You can't do that!"

"Are you testing me?" the judge asked, narrowing her eyes at Priscilla. "Because you can join her in jail for ninety days."

Priscilla had enough sense to promptly clamp her mouth shut. "No ma'am."

"That's what I thought," the judge said.

"Your honor," Faye spoke up again. "My client would also like full custody of Maggie–"

"You must be out of your mind!" Priscilla shouted. "Absolutely not!"

""It's not like you're the one who takes care of her!" Cyn shouted back. "You don't even know where her food is."

"Order!" the judge called out. "Who is Maggie?"

"My dog!" Priscilla cried.

The judge leaned forwards as she asked, "And *does* she take care of the dog the majority of the time?"

"Well…yeah. But it's her job," Priscilla weakly argued.

"I see…Miss Tremaine is to receive the inheritance that was promised to her in her father, Frank Tremaine's will. I'm also granting her full custody of Maggie the dog. Court is adjourned."

The judge banged her gavel, stood and we all followed suit.

Cyn wrapped her arms around Faye for a hug and then turned and came over to me.

"Well, that was..."

"Insane?" Cyn finished my sentence.

"Yeah. To say the least," I replied. "But it seems like the worst is over."

"I think so too."

Faye came over and looped her arm through Cyn's. "Sorry, but I need to steal her away for a few minutes."

"Sure thing," I said, and watched as they disappeared into the crowd filled with people.

I left the courtroom and hung out in the lobby until Cyn and Faye came out, Cyn looking lighter than I'd ever seen her.

I took her hand in mine and we left the courthouse.

"What would you like to do?" I asked as I lifted my free hand in the air to hail a taxi. "You wanna go out and celebrate?"

She had *a lot* of reasons to. Over half a million reasons to be precise. And that didn't even include whatever she stood to make once she sold off her shares.

Cyn shook her head and then rested it on my shoulder. "I just want to go home."

"Home it is then," I said as I opened the taxi door that had just pulled up. I followed her into the cab, gave the driver Cyn's address and we were off.

The drive from the courthouse to Cyn's apartment wasn't too long and we didn't say much. I paid the driver when he dropped us off and then we went up to Cyn's place.

We went inside and went over to the couch, where we both sat down.

"You okay?" I asked her.

"Yeah, just glad to be done with all this bullshit," Cyn said, sliding one of her feet out of her platform heel. I reached down and grabbed her other foot and took the shoe off and began massaging her feet. "Mmmm, that feels good. I could get use to the this. You're gonna spoil me with this kind of stuff."

"Maybe someday we'll be able to make this a regular occurrence."

"What if that 'someday' was sooner rather than later?"

I stopped massaging Cyn's feet and looked up at her.

Cyn pulled her feet away from my hands and tucked them beneath her. "I...I spoke with Izzy the last night I was in Sweet Rapids. She'd gotten a glimpse of my sketchbook one day and was highly impressed. So much so that she told me if I ever considered bringing my work to life, I had a job waiting for me at her fashion house if I wanted."

"Really?"

"Yeah," Cyn said, nodding her head.

Excitement rushed through me as I looked her in the eyes.

"Are you going to take the job?"

"I booked a flight to go back to Sweet Rapids this weekend."

"Wow. That's *soon* soon."

"I know. I've got so much to figure out," I watched as Cyn stood up and walked over to the door that led out to her balcony. "I never thought I'd love a place any more than I loved New York, but there was just something about Nevada, Sweet Rapids in particular, that just felt like...home."

I stood and walked over to her.

"Yeah, I remember feeling the same way when we moved there. The place leaves its mark on you."

"And so do the people," Cyn said, turning to face me.

"Is that right? Any person in particular?" I teased and Cyn threw her head back and laughed.

"Well there's this photographer guy," she said, closing the distance between us. She wrapped her arms around my neck.

My lip quirked up as I rested my hands on her waist. "Oh yeah?"

"Yes." She rose on her tiptoes and lifted her mouth to meet mine in a kiss. "Roman, you came into my life at...the exact right time that I needed you and I didn't even know it. You're like...a real life prince charming or something."

I grinned at her and shook my head. "I definitely ain't no prince charming, gorgeous. Way too wild for that kind of shit. But I've gotta admit, I am excited that you'll be moving to Sweet Rapids."

"You are?" Cyn asked, smiling brightly at me.

"Absolutely," I replied.

She let out a peal of laughter, when I picked her up, tossed her over my shoulder and carried her off to the bedroom to show her just how excited I was.

The End...

ACKNOWLEDGMENTS

Thank you to Nicole, Bailey, Danielle, Alex, AmberLynn and Christina for all of your encouragement and for listening to me whine, and complain and cry my eyes out over this book. And also for staying on my ass and helping me stay focused. Y'all rock.

ALSO BY TÉ RUSS

<u>Standalone</u>

Love by the Books

Santa Baby (A Holiday Short)

Runaway Love

Gingerbread Wishes (A Holiday Short)

Live at Five: A Té Russ Short

<u>McAllister Friends</u>

Dream Lover

Taking Chances

Always You

<u>McAllister Family Series</u>

After the Storm

Just One Kiss

Perfection

Love After War

Just One Night

Just Once Touch

Reckless Love (A McAllister Family/McAllister Security Crossover)

<u>The Coalton, Texas Novella Series</u>

Homecoming

Sanctuary

Reawakening

Destined

Irresistible

Four Seasons of Love Series

A Spring Affair

Sultry Summer Nights

Autumn Kisses

A Winter Rendezvous

In the Line of Love Series

Let Me Love You

Love's Taken Over

In the Line of Love: Fire & Rescue

Piece of My Love

The Nobles of Sweet Rapids

Noble Love

Noble Surrender

Noble Redemption

Noble Seduction

McAllister Security

Reckless Love (A McAllister Family/McAllister Security Crossover)

Dangerous Love

Vigilant Love

Lessons in Love: A Series Collaboration with Nicole Falls and Bailey West

Acting on Love

The Wild Knights

Falling for a Knight

Seduced by a Knight (2019)

Claimed by a Knight (2019)

ABOUT THE AUTHOR

Té Russ is a contemporary romance author who focuses on stories centered around black love. With over 30 projects under her belt, she continues to bring soulful tales to life. In addition to writing, Té is also a certified aerial yoga instructor and teaches at a local studio. She enjoys spending her free time with her family, baking or reading.

KEEP IN TOUCH!

Facebook: www.facebook.com/TeRussNovels & www.facebook.com/TeRussAuthor
Twitter: www.twitter.com/TeRussNovels
Blog: www.terussnovels.blogspot.com
Email: terussnovels@gmail.com